COMBATANTS WILL BE DISPATCHED
5
"What, are we fighting? You know I don't back down when it comes to food."
ROSE
A Chimera who can copy the abilities of any monster she eats, just like K*rby. Now formally a Kisaragi Combat Agent Recruit.
ROSE'S VIEW
Since I've been eating nothing but mokemokes in the woods lately, my finger scissors can even break rocks.
THIS VOLUME'S MAIN HEROINE

"Barkeep! I'll have one of everything on the menu!"

"Don't worry, Boss. There won't be anything left as long as I'm here!"

"You're one to talk! You always order the most expensive drinks on my tab!"

THE "NIGHT BEFORE BATTLE" EVENT

ALICE KISARAGI

"Just because I'm paying doesn't mean it's all-you-can-eat!"

"I heard humans are supposed to mature as they grow older, but you all never change."

AGENT SIX

"Welcome, brave yet foolhardy humans... In acknowledgment of the courage it took for you to appear before me, I shall grant you all swift and painless deaths..."

VIPER

The mysterious beauty in the Demon Lord's audience chamber. The Demon Lord's supposed to be a middle-aged dude, isn't he...?

THE "DEMON LORD'S CASTLE" EVENT

■VIPER'S VIEW
Um... A-all right, I understand...
One more time, then...

"Sorry, I didn't quite catch that. From the top, please."

"Yeah, I need to hear that again. I'll record it this time, so go ahead."

TILLIS'S VIEW
Please don't. Seriously, please, please don't.

"You've really done it this time, you moron. I told you to stay put, but *nooo*. You couldn't even trust your own partner, huh?"

THE "EVIL-ORGANIZATION INFIGHTING" EVENT

"Sorry, Alice, I need you to back down this time. Otherwise, I'm gonna use my points to turn this kingdom into a sea of flames."

CONTENTS

//

Prologue
P. 001

Chapter 1   The Girl Who Welcomes Death   P. 005

Chapter 2   It's Usually the Boss's Fault   P. 043

Chapter 3   My Hobby Is Solving Puzzles
             in Video Games   P. 073

Chapter 4   Vs. the Sand King   P. 111

Final Chapter   A Celebration of Villainy   P. 147

Epilogue
P. 199

COMBATANTS WILL BE DISPATCHED!

COMBATANTS WILL BE DISPATCHED!

5

Natsume Akatsuki

ILLUSTRATION BY
Kakao Lanthanum

YEN
ON
NEW YORK

COMBATANTS WILL BE DISPATCHED!

Natsume Akatsuki

5

Translation by Noboru Akimoto
Cover art by Kakao Lanthanum

SENTOIN, HAKEN SHIMASU! Volume 5
© Natsume Akatsuki, Kakao • Lanthanum 2020
First published in Japan in 2020 by KADOKAWA CORPORATION, Tokyo.
English translation rights arranged with KADOKAWA CORPORATION, Tokyo through
TUTTLE-MORI AGENCY, INC., Tokyo.

English translation © 2021 by Yen Press, LLC

Yen On
150 West 30th Street, 19th Floor
New York, NY 10001

Visit us at yenpress.com
facebook.com/yenpress
twitter.com/yenpress
yenpress.tumblr.com
instagram.com/yenpress

First Yen On Edition: March 2021

Yen On is an imprint of Yen Press, LLC.
The Yen On name and logo are trademarks of Yen Press, LLC.

Library of Congress Cataloging-in-Publication Data
Names: Akatsuki, Natsume, author. | Lanthanum, Kakao, illustrator. | Akimoto, Noboru, translator.
Title: Combatants will be dispatched! / Natsume Akatsuki ; illustration by Kakao Lanthanum ; translation by
    Noboru Akimoto ; cover art by Kakao Lanthanum.
Other titles: Sentoin haken shimasu!. English
Description: First Yen On edition. | New York : Yen On, 2019.
Identifiers: LCCN 2019025056 | ISBN 9781975385583 (v. 1 ; trade paperback) |
    ISBN 9781975331528 (v. 2 ; trade paperback) | ISBN 9781975399023 (v. 3 ; trade paperback) |
    ISBN 9781975313685 (v. 4 ; trade paperback)) | ISBN 9781975316556 (v. 5 ; trade paperback)
Subjects: CYAC: Science fiction. | Robots—Fiction.
Classification: LCC PZ7.1.A38 Se 2019 | DDC [Fic]—dc23
LC record available at https://lccn.loc.gov/2019025056

ISBNs: 978-1-9753-1655-6 (paperback)
978-1-9753-1656-3 (ebook)

10 9 8 7 6 5 4 3 2 1

LSC-C

Printed in the United States of America

Prologue

Astaroth's voice echoes throughout Kisaragi headquarters.

"For the last time. You don't need to follow Lilith's orders! Leave the local mission to another Combat Agent and come home!"

"Even if you say that, we have to follow procedures, ma'am. The only person who can rescind an order given by a Supreme Leader is that same Supreme Leader. That's just protocol, y'know?"

Astaroth's brow twitches as Six refuses the order from the other side of the monitor, casually picking his nose in the process.

"You don't know the first thing about protocol! Someone must have fed you that line! Alice told you to say that, didn't she? …Go on, Lilith, cancel your order."

Looks like the self-righteous Astaroth still wants to preserve her rule-abiding-leader façade.

"Heya, Six. Sorry, the order I gave is canceled. You can come back to Earth now."

Well…that was anticlimactic.

"Nah, I'm good. Lady Lilith, you're tied up and hanging upside down. You're obviously being coerced into rescinding the order.

But don't worry. I'm your loyal subordinate, and I understand the circumstances. Leave it to me."

"H-hold it! There's a reason Lilith's hog-tied like this. I'm not threatening her..."

"You're right, Six! Astaroth and Belial are bullying me! They took my treasure, and now they've hog-tied me and are tortur— *Mrrph...!*"

Astaroth quickly claps a hand over Lilith's mouth, causing Six to gasp.

"I thought Lady Lilith did something dumb and got herself into that situation, but to think she's actually being coerced...! Not to worry, Lady Lilith, I will continue my assignment until you can prove to me that you're safe and sound, so please don't give in to the machinations of the Evil Femme Fatale!"

"She's one of those Evil Femme Fatales, you know! W-wait...hold on...!"

After making his declaration, Six cuts the line without waiting for a response.

The control room is engulfed in silence, with Lilith hanging hog-tied from the ceiling and a shocked Astaroth staring at the blank screen.

Lilith flashes a spiteful grin at her.

"Things seem pretty dire, Astaroth. Looks like Six isn't coming home anytime soon. Though, there is one way to change that. I can go over there again myself and directly rescind the order. Can't do it over a monitor. It's our MO to hide threatening weapons off-screen, after all."

"......"

In the face of the trussed-up Lilith's gloating, Astaroth remains unmoved.

"Whether or not I cooperate on bringing Six back depends on your attitude. Heh-heh-heh... Oh, how the tables have turned! Now then, my demands are threefold. First, return my tentacles and all my hard-won loot. Second, treat me with the respect a genius scientist like myself deserves. That means no more hog-tying even when I screw up. And third—"

"The loot you brought back isn't here."

"—I want one day off a week… Wait, what'd you just say?"

Lilith stops wriggling in her bonds for a moment.

Astaroth gestures to the control room.

"Look around. You and I are the only two here. Your spoils are with Belial. She mentioned something about rewarding all her underlings."

"…Untie me! Please, Astaroth, I'll help you talk Six into coming back! Just untie me! All the effort I put in on that planet is about to go up in smoke!"

As Lilith squirms and desperately pleads to Astaroth, an announcement comes in over the Kisaragi intercom.

"Attention, all mutants and Combat Agents currently here at headquarters. Lady Belial will be treating everyone to dinner and drinks. Those on nonessential tasks are to gather at the lobby. Those completing essential tasks, please make your way to the party venue as soon as you're able…"

"Look, Astaroth, it was all my fault, okay? Hurry! I'm sorry I taunted you last time! A lot happened on that planet, but I worked my ass off! Also, I really need to pee! I've been holding it in for longer than I care to mention!"

Sweat beads on Lilith's brow as she cries out, but Astaroth simply ignores her, gazing up at the sky through the window.

"Come home soon, you big dummy…"

"Stop getting sentimental and untie me already! The dam's gonna burst!"

CHAPTER 1

The Girl Who Welcomes Death

1

It's been one week since Lilith the Black bombed the defense facilities of the Demon Lord's Castle.

Lilith, despite showing up with lots of flashy Earth tech in the hope of wowing the locals into subservience, didn't actually do a whole lot, threw a tantrum, and ended up invading demon territory.

It was believed the Demon Lord's Army would swiftly open negotiations after being subjected to the overwhelming firepower of a Kisaragi Supreme Leader, but we have yet to hear from Heine.

Plus, with Lilith back on Earth, it'd be difficult to attack the Demon Lord's Castle again anytime soon.

Which is why, with nothing to do, we've been chatting in the base's rec room, but…

"Hey, Six, look at this!"

Snow suddenly bursts through the door while I'm playing with a video-game console Lilith brought from Earth.

Holding out what appears to be a report of some kind, Snow says in her self-aggrandizing tone:

"I, the capable one, have brought you information about the Demon Lord! Everything from the Demon Lord's hobbies, gender, special abilities, to even his favorite foods! Go and make use of my information in your negotiations!"

After reading through a bit of Snow's report, I crumple it up and toss it over my shoulder.

"Wh-what are you doing?!"

"That's what I should be asking you! What the hell, Snow?! Judging by everything we've been through so far, it only makes sense for the Demon Lord to be a beautiful woman or a pretty girl! And she's supposed to use the royal *we* and have some archaic accent or something! Kisaragi's Supreme Leaders are all women! Why? Because that's how it's supposed to be! So..."

In spite of all that...

"...why the hell does your report say the Demon Lord is some middle-aged dude?!"

"How should I know?! And why would the Demon Lord be a woman? The Supreme Leaders might all be women where you're from, but most rulers here are men! Go on, read the rest!"

Sighing, I start reading the sheet of paper as it's uncrumpled and shoved into my face.

"'The Demon Lord Mehlmehl: a powerful being who has ruled over the demon territory for the last two hundred years. He appears to be a middle-aged man with horns. He originally maintained a reasonable distance from humanity, but having had much of his territory turned into desert by the giant monster known as the Sand King, he suddenly began an invasion of the kingdom of Grace. After a long period of war that saw both the Demon Lord's Army and the human army suffer heavy losses, the royal seer prophesized the awakening of the Chosen One, the death of the Demon Lord, and the arrival of a short-term peace for humanity. However, the Chosen One appears to be missing in action, and the seer was fired for giving inaccurate predictions...'

"...Hey, this part about the seer getting fired bothers me. If Alice and I hadn't shown up, the prophecy might not have been wrong."

The Chosen One should've been the one to defeat the Demon Lord, just like in the stories.

Adding an irregular element to the mix (namely us) seems to have thrown things out of whack.

...I mean, this planet just happens to closely resemble a fantasy world. It's not like we're actually in a video game or a novel, so it's probably fine if things aren't totally by the book.

Still, I feel a little guilty about it...

"You say that, but the seer's already been banished. Besides, why should we believe in some sketchy prophecy? When the seer was still around, they couldn't even properly forecast the price of commodity futures!"

"You're a real piece of work, you know that...? We've always had our hands full fighting for survival. Let's leave the past in the past."

If I ever run into the seer, I'll apologize and buy them a cup of coffee.

Putting that aside...

"'He has an arrogant, greedy personality, but he is dedicated to securing prosperity for the demons. The invasion should have demonstrated our power to the demons, so if we hint at the risks to his people, we should have an advantage in negotiations...' You *are* a knight, right? You're not actually part of an evil organization like us, are you?"

Snow's notes sound awfully similar to something you'd read in a Kisaragi report.

I've always thought she was shady, but this is enough to turn me off.

"It's precisely because I am a knight of this kingdom. I put my nation before any other and pray death swiftly befalls my enemies. When you meet the Demon Lord, you should try that line of questioning on him. I have no doubt he'll answer the same way. As I was doing my research, I couldn't help but feel a certain kinship with him…"

Wow, she really was sympathizing with the Demon Lord…

For the sake of this country, maybe I should do something about her first.

At least she's hot. I bet she'd make a good hostess.

But just as I consider knocking her out from behind and sending her to one of the Kisaragi-run hostess clubs on Earth…

"Oh, there you are. I was wondering where you'd disappeared to. If you're not doing anything, come lend me a hand."

…Alice appears in the rec-room doorway, shotgun and backpack in tow.

Previously, Supreme Leader Lilith had ordered:

"You two are to begin espionage and invasion preparations on the surrounding kingdoms, using this hideout as your base."

She'd also said:

"In parallel, you will be responsible for founding a city capable of supporting human life in this area, with this fortress at its center. Bring life back to these wastelands, tame those woods, and create a foundation for settling earthlings on this planet!"

Since we haven't taken care of the Demon Lord problem, we can't start spying on surrounding kingdoms.

Meaning the only work we can do at the moment is the other task: settling this forest…

"Six, the treants are headed your way! Not only are they a great source of lumber, but their leaves can be sold as magic supplies! Don't let them get by you!"

"Yeah right! I'm a Combat Agent, not a lumberjack!"

I'm currently with Alice and Snow in the woods near our base.

"Don't be like that, partner. We're seriously short on building materials. We gotta save up on Evil Points. I'll give you some spending money when we're done, all right?"

"Don't think you can just buy me off with spending money every time! I'm only taking gold coins! Shiny ones at that!"

As the trees—er, treants run away using their roots as legs, I ready my R-Buzzsaw.

Treants are the walking-tree creatures you occasionally see in fantasy games and stuff.

I've given up dwelling on the weird creatures on this planet. It's pointless to question why trees would move around.

It's a world with magic, after all. There might even be a world with killer vegetables somewhere in this vast universe.

As I struggle with the injustice of this planet's ecosystem, Snow calls out from behind.

"Wait, Six! If there's a steady supply of gold coins to be had, I'll take up woodcutting!"

"A-are you serious?! If you ditch the whole knight thing, your boobs'll be the only positive trait you have left! ...Hey, there's something in the trees!"

As I turn around in exasperation, I notice one of the trees has a bunch of round things stuck to it that resemble black ping-pong balls.

"...Hmm? Ah, mipyokopyoko eggs. Great, let's grab them."

Snow then goes to casually pick them up, but I seem to recall that name being...

"Hold on, aren't mipyokopyokos the things that blow up? What are you going to do with the eggs of a creature that dangerous?"

"Mipyokopyoko eggs won't explode if you don't subject them to shock. You can use them as weapons and throw them at enemies. And if you dry them out and grind them into powder, they become a potent fire starter. In other words, they're valuable."

Man, she really does have money on the brain twenty-four seven.

"Don't leave them in your room at the hideout and accidentally hatch them."

"I'd never do something that stupid. These don't hatch unless they're exposed to pure moonlight for an extended period of time. Nothing will happen if you leave them in the dark."

Still, between treants, mokemokes, and these tongue-twister mystery monsters, this world really is full of weird creatures.

As I grab the mipyokopyoko eggs, my mind wanders.

"Hey, morons! The treants are getting away!"

""Oh.""

A while later, Alice addresses us in front of the pile of lumber in the hideout's storehouse.

"Well done, you two. Here's your payment. Remember, we have more to do tomorrow."

With the war against the Demon Lord's Army suspended, all available Combat Agents other than me are off gathering materials.

In the storehouse, there's also stone from the mountains and piles of ores.

"Whoo-hoo, a shiny gold coin! I'm gonna drown in booze tonight!"

"Hey, Six. If you're going drinking, I'm sure you wouldn't mind having this peerless beauty accompany you."

After receiving my pay from Alice, who looks all of twelve years old, I'm in a pretty good mood.

"Screw that! You're just planning to leech off me, aren't you?! 'Peerless beauty' my ass. Now that I know what you're like on the inside, I barely consider you a lady!"

"Heh-heh, you clearly don't know anything about women. Having a tiny flaw or two makes us more relatable and approachable."

Your issues are just as huge as your tits.

"Look, if you buy me dinner, I'll pour your drinks for you! I've been in survival mode for so long that I really miss eating out!"

"You just got a gold coin! Treat yourself! And what do you mean by 'survival mode'? ...Wait. You *did* get your coin, didn't you?"

Hang on a sec, did Alice only pay me?

Hearing my question, Alice looks over while wearing an expression that seems to say, *Of course.*

"For now, I'm funneling Snow's income into paying off her loans."

"Which is why, to reduce my living expenses as much as possible, I've been gathering things that seem edible from the woods. You're my commander, remember? You have to make sure your troops stay fed!"

The former captain of the Royal Guard has sure fallen far.

"Oh, so I'm your commander again, am I? Just the other day, you were talking about how you wanted nothing to do with me... Hey, there's no point in shoving your boobs up against me. I can't feel them through my power armor."

Snow has been firmly pressing her chest against my arm, but discovering her advances aren't very effective, she gives herself a squeeze instead.

"You bastard... I remember how you ogled me when we first met! What the hell? Have you found a new target to harass? Are you seriously going to claim you've found someone better?! I'm pretty confident in these! They're the best breasts in the kingdom, if I say so myself! Commander, please! Feed your poor, starving soldier!"

"J-just how far are you going to fall...? I'll buy you dinner, so stop feeling yourself up already..."

Ordinarily, I'd shut up and enjoy the show, but this is just too sad to consider sexy.

Watching my pitiable subordinate celebrate, something else comes to mind.

"Hey, speaking of troops, what are Rose and Grimm up to?"

"Those two did their daily training at the castle, then went to seek an audience with Princess Tillis. They mentioned wanting to discuss the future…"

Well, I guess those two are technically soldiers of this kingdom.

And while Rose formally became a Combat Agent Recruit the other day, she hasn't signed the contracts for her salary and other matters yet.

Wait…

"Those two are working, but you, the knight, are off making money on side jobs?"

"It seems you've forgotten my job is to keep an eye on you. And a knight's role during peacetime is to preserve that peace. That means watching after you troublemakers is my responsibility. In other words, this is my top priority, not a side hustle."

Snow says this with a serious expression as she busily stuffs the eggs she plundered into a bag.

2

That night.

"Barkeep! I'll have one of everything on the menu!"

"Not so fast, Lady Whitemane! Just because I'm paying doesn't mean it's all-you-can-eat!"

"You're one to talk! You always order the most expensive drinks on my tab!"

In the bar where we first had drinks with Snow shortly after landing on this rock, Alice and the rest of my squad have joined me for a rare happy hour.

I take a long swig from a mug of beer as Grimm grabs and shakes me by the shoulder. Rose raises a fist while munching on some bar snacks.

"Don't worry, Boss. There won't be anything left as long as I'm here!"

"I'm not worried about that. I'm worried about the contents of my wallet. With a group this large, it's gonna be hard to sneak out."

"Commander, I'm begging you not to dine and dash! This is one of my regular bars!"

Grimm punctuates this by banging her hands on the table, and Alice says something faintly nostalgic as she watches us.

"I heard humans are supposed to mature as they grow older, but you all never change."

"In other words, you're saying we're forever young. I can take that as a compliment, right?"

Uh, probably not.

Just then, Rose, who's been snacking away, straightens her back as though she's come to a decision.

"...Boss, Ms. Alice, I have something to tell you."

"Hmm? You want our snacks, too? *Sigh.* Fine, knock yourself out."

"I can't eat, so you can have mine, too. Here ya go."

"No, that's not it! I mean, I'll still take them, but...!"

While moving the snack plates to her corner of the table, Rose hardens her expression as she continues:

"I've officially resigned from the Grace Kingdom army. From now on, I'll do my best as a Kisaragi Combat Agent! Thanks for giving me this opportunity!"

"Whaa—?!"

Snow yelps in surprise as Grimm smiles happily.

"I still have some duties to hand over as a high-ranking member of my order, but my resignation will be effective as of next month, too. You're short on hands, right? I'm sure an Archbishop of Zenarith will be very useful to have around."

"Grimm, not you too!"

Snow reels in shock while Alice and I exchange whispers...

"Um, Alice, I know we've been pushing Rose as a mutant candidate, but what do we do about Grimm?"

"Let's be honest. Is there really any demand for a wheelchair-bound Combat Agent? She'll have pretty significant terrain restrictions, so we should probably just station her in this country for the most part and then wheel her out when she's needed..."

"I can hear you, you know! Hold on a moment. I showed you how useful I can be during the Undead Festival, didn't I?! Sure, I'm usually pretty useless, but I'm an asset when it counts! B-besides...!"

Grimm gives me a meaningful glance.

"Besides, isn't a girl with a few flaws a little cuter than some perfect woman?"

"You're sounding like Snow now."

Grimm freezes at my remark, and Snow rubs her temples at the idea of the two of them quitting.

Rose lets out a bashful chuckle and paws at the back of her head.

"Even as a Recruit, I'll be working for Kisaragi from now on, so I thought I needed to clarify where I stand. Which is why I made sure to tell Princess Tillis."

"F-for my part, I couldn't just leave Rose on her own, you know! And also you, Commander! You're weirdly vulnerable at times! You have no problem with me joining, right? Because I'll be unemployed otherwise! I already handed in my resignation for next month!"

Grimm seems more than a little clingy while saying this, but I suppose it's her way of looking out for Rose.

"...Well, I suppose we can do that. I mean, you've got that weird mystery power that makes you useful at times. Besides, we don't have a mutant zombie-woman yet. I'm also not gonna complain about having another female subordinate."

"Welcome to the team, then, Mutant Zombie-Woman! Since I'm your superior now, you better show me respect! Make sure you call me Ms. Alice."

"Don't call me that! I'll curse you!"

With the addition of Mutant Zombie-Woman settled, we're about to do another round of toasts when...

...Snow slams her empty mug onto the table and glares at us.

"...Hrmph! Just this once, I'll ignore the fact that you headhunted Rose and Grimm from our country. I hate to say it, but they were treated like garbage before you arrived. I don't have any right to stand in the way of their happiness when they're this excited. HOWEVER—!"

"Depending on what you say next, you might be paying your own tab."

Snow's momentum comes to a screeching halt.

"...H-however...I won't be so easily pulled away from my duty! I may be easily bribed, but my loyalty to this kingdom is..."

Her words trickle out, and Alice and I exchange glances.

"Even I know it'd be a bad idea to try to recruit a loyal knight."

"We can just leave Snow where she is. She can look after the kingdom and come do side gigs for us when we need her."

"Hwaaah?!"

Snow's weird utterance confirms we caught her completely off guard.

"I mean, thinking about it, I guess I'm also employed by the kingdom. Since things are gonna get pretty busy on the Kisaragi side, should I also have a chat with Tillis?"

"In your case, your employment is part of maintaining relations with this country. I don't think it's a problem for you to keep pulling double salary from Kisaragi and the local regime. So there ya have it, Snow. We're not gonna force you to join us; you can relax."

Hearing that, Rose excitedly tugs on Alice's sleeve.

"Ms. Alice, Ms. Alice, I recall being aggressively coerced into becoming a Combat Agent Recruit..."

"Hey, here comes the food we ordered. I don't eat, so you can go ahead and have my share."

"Yay! Thank you!"

As Rose is drawn away from her memory by the sight of food, Snow starts rapidly laying out her case.

"Y-you really aren't going to try to recruit me?! I mean, I'm still a former member of the Royal Guard, if nothing else. Hell, I was the captain! I've got leadership skills and plenty of fighting ability. Are you sure you want to give up on me so quickly?"

For some reason, Snow seems to be in a slight panic.

"We've got plenty of guys who can fight. Hey, Rose, gimme some of whatever that is... Is it some sort of stewed lizard?"

"This is stewed mupyokopyoko. It has this delicious *pop* flavor."

What sort of flavor is "pop" exactly? It doesn't explode, does it?

"Y-you're okay with this, then?! My network of informants is quite impressive! You'll regret letting me go!"

"I keep telling you we don't need you! We've got Alice, and I'm pretty sure she's much better at gathering intel than you are. I mean, she's hooked up to a satellite, for crying out loud. All the knowledge of this world is laid bare before her!"

As I taunt her, Snow's brow twitches violently...

"Yo, Six, with Lady Lilith gone, we don't have access to the military satellites anymore."

Alice mentions that supremely valuable fact as though we're just swapping gossip.

"Huh? Why?! Isn't the satellite still in orbit? Why can't we use it anymore?"

"No clue. Last picture it took showed something like a floating island. Since we didn't see anything like that when we arrived, it might've been hidden with optical camo."

A mysterious floating island that shoots down satellites in space...

"Oh, so it seems you can't use Alice's secret weapon after all! Well then, I wouldn't be opposed to lending you my network in exchange for a not-so-modest fee, and perhaps a little groveling? Bwa-ha-ha-ha-ha!"

Snow wraps her arm around my shoulder, more smug than she has any right to be.

"What the hell is up with this planet anyway? It's full of screwball creatures like giant sparrows and giant moles! And the people are just as weird!"

"Six, you better not be including me among those weird people! Just admit it already! You need my abilities! Go on, say it! You want me!"

What the hell? Snow's being way more of a pain in my ass than usual.

"You've gotta be— Did you seriously chug your drink even though you're a lightweight?! Grimm, she's cut off!"

Despite her usual stubbornness and arrogance, Snow's as bad at holding her liquor as anyone else her age.

When we were running our scam hostess club, we even had to prepare nonalcoholic drinks just for her...

"I'm not a lightweight! Look, my mug's empty! I can drink as much as I want!"

"Well said, Snow! You can drink with the best of them! What a woman! Now drink this next."

"I said, she's cut off! She lives at the hideout right now! You know who has to drag her back, right?!"

"Boff! If you're nah eafing thif meat, can I haf if?"

Snow turns beet-red from the alcohol while desperately trying to convince us that she's not three sheets to the wind. Grimm, wildly amused by the spectacle, funnels her more drinks. Rose just chows down without a care in a world. It's all so familiar to another night in recent memory.

"You better be able to walk home! Otherwise, I'm just gonna toss you into a cheap inn and leave you there!"

"You're going to push me down in a cheap inn? You hear that, Grimm? He plans to have his way with me! Ah-ha! So *that's* why you're trying to get me drunk! Pervert!"

"I said I'm leaving you there! And you only have yourself to blame for your drunkenness! And stop acting like I'd just throw myself at any woman I saw!"

As we get into a shoving match, Grimm laughs and downs her drink while Rose starts cheering us on to keep fighting.

Alice then chimes in with amused exasperation.

"You guys really don't change…"

"Um, excuse me, I know you're valued customers, but could you please knock it off already…?" says a nearby server.

3

I ended up carrying Snow back to the hideout last night after she begged, through drunken sobs, not to be the only one left out. Which brings us to today…

"…Good morning…"

While I'm sitting in the cafeteria reading a translated newspaper and eating breakfast, a red-faced Snow wanders in.

Judging by her unusually docile behavior, it seems she remembers her drunken antics.

As Snow fitfully sends tiny glances in my direction…

"Mornin', sunshine. Looks like somebody had a little too much fun last night, huh?"

"K-kill me already!"

Snow drops to her knees while performing a double facepalm as I sip my miso soup and continue perusing the paper.

"'…Sand King rapidly expanding territory. Caravan merchants

are warned to take extra precautions. Our paper also helps provide arrangements with mercenary units; for details, contact us at…'"

…Huh, I didn't even know there were mercenary units in this country.

They're industry competitors of a different sort from the Demon Lord's Army. We should probably go have a chat with them sometime.

Just as I'm thinking up Kisaragi-style "negotiation" techniques…

"Ah, Six, mornin'."

…Alice walks into the cafeteria, directing an amused look over to Snow.

"Oh, and good morning to our dear Snow, who threw a tantrum while saying things like, *'I don't want to go home yet!'* and *'I'm part of your team, right? Don't abandon me!'* then passed out from crying too much."

"How much…? If you forget about last night, I'll happily agree to any amount you add to my debt…"

As Snow mutters in a shaky voice, Alice casually remarks:

"Androids never forget, I'm afraid. But don't worry about that. Come with me to the castle. It looks like the emissary from the Demon Lord's Army is finally here."

It's been a while since I've been to the palace, and things look quite a bit different on the outside.

There are countless spear-shaped objects buried atop the outer wall, as well as a large, newly constructed moat.

"Huh, I didn't realize they redecorated the castle. I didn't think Tillis was the sort of person to shell out for something like this."

"You do realize you're the cause, right? This is all because you and your ilk kept breaking into Her Highness's room."

…Ohhh, that makes sense. Ten and I did sneak in pretty often.

What a shame. That was a gold mine of Evil Points…

"What are you looking at? Also, make sure you tell your fellow perverts to stay the hell out!"

We have so many perverts at Kisaragi that I'm not quite sure where to start.

I mean, if you exclude me, the only gentleman, we're pretty much all perverts.

"Yeah, they're perverts, all right, but they don't mean any harm. Could you let them off the hook? For me? Anyway, let's make sure Heine gets an earful for keeping us waiting for so long."

"Y-you seriously don't believe you're any different from the others?"

Hearing that, Alice, who's been leading the charge, stops and turns back to face us.

"Looks like Heine's not the emissary. It's another young woman, so try to keep your hands to yourself."

Oh hey, I wonder if that means I'm allowed a little wiggle room.

…When we reach the castle gate, one of the soldiers notices us and opens it up.

"Welcome, Lady Alice. Sir Six. Right this way."

As we begin following the soldier, I hear Snow yelling behind us.

"What is the meaning of this?!"

"I'm afraid our orders are to only allow Lady Alice and Sir Six inside…"

When I turn around, I see a soldier barring Snow's entry.

"D-don't be ridiculous! I'm a knight of this realm! Not only that, but I'm the former captain of the Royal Guard and a retainer of Princess Tillis! Are you a new recruit who's never seen me before?! I'll ignore that insult this time, but don't let it happen again!"

With that, Snow tries to shove her way through, but the soldier doesn't budge.

"I know who you are, Lady Snow. I'm sorry to be the bearer of bad news…"

"Yes, we've, um…been told to only allow you in if it's an emergency…"

"What?! Why?!"

I guess Snow's recent string of screwups has come back to bite her.

"How dare you expendables mock me! I'll show you what it means to denigrate a knight!"

"Oh no, she's drawn her blade! Call for backup!"

"This one's no longer a knight, just a common criminal! Apprehend her!"

Ignoring the bustle behind us, Alice and I decide to go join Tillis—

"…Sir Six, Ms. Alice, my apologies for the sudden summons. The Demon Lord's emissary has arrived…"

I suppose you could call it the castle's salon.

Inside the spacious room are some expensive-looking sofas, and sitting across from Tillis is a winged demon girl.

She seems friendly enough. She stands when she notices us.

"It's a pleasure to meet you. My name is Camille. I am a dream demon and longtime servant of the Demon Lord. I've been tasked with serving as the representative in the cease-fire negotiations with the kingdom of Grace."

Camille then bows deeply.

"I'm the Kisaragi Corporation's negotiator, Miss Alice Kisaragi. Nice to meet ya."

Alice's introduction is brief. While the other party might be a young woman, we can't very well afford to be underestimated by an industry rival.

I stick my hands in my pockets, look her up and down, and glare.

"Yo, I'm the Kisaragi rep in charge of things around here. You could say we're a mercenary group of sorts. The name's Six. Mr. Combat Agent Six…"

…Wait, back up. Did she just introduce herself as—?

"...Did you just say you were a dream demon? Like...one of *those* demons who let you have really sexy dreams? Are you a succubus or something?"

"N-no, I'm afraid I'm slightly different from a succubus. I'm a Lilim, and while we do use dreams to tempt people, much like a succubus, the dreams we conjure aren't, um, the erotic kind..."

Camille seems a lot more normal than the weirdos we've encountered so far. Even the mention of sexy dreams makes her blush faintly as she continues her explanation.

"So you're in the same line of work as succubi, but you don't deal in sexy dreams... A succubus downgrade, in other words."

"N-not at all! We're not inferior! In fact, we Lilim are the very first demons birthed by the Mother of All Demons herself: the Great Demon Lilith! We're her chosen children! True elites!"

...

"<Alice! Aliiiice! Did you just hear what she said?! She's Lady Lilith's daughter! What the hell?! Who's her dad, then?!>"

"<Calm down, Six. We'll make sure to file a proper report. But you know, the phrase *Mother of All Demons* is really similar to Lady Lilith's habit of calling herself the 'mother of all mutants.' With that much of a similarity, it can't be a coincidence. Let's have the other Supreme Leaders ask her directly.>"

Camille tilts her head in confusion when she hears us speaking Japanese.

"Sorry about that; the unexpected information threw me off a moment. Let's get back on topic. What were you saying about boobs?"

"That word hasn't come up at all! What is wrong with you?! Are you enjoying mocking me?!"

As Camille starts raising her voice, Tillis holds up her hands to calm her down.

"Despite their eccentricities, their strength is the real deal. After all, Sir Six is the one who defeated the Elite Four pillar, Gadalkand of the Earth."

"This is the man who took down Lord Gadalkand…," says Camille in surprise, her eyes going wide.

"Hold on, that happened in battle. You're not gonna bring that up now, are you? We've had plenty of soldiers killed by you guys, too."

"No, we understand and have no intention of raising it as an issue… I see. So you're the one Lady Heine mentioned…"

At the sudden mention of Heine's name, I can't help but ask:

"What did she say about me? By my calculations, it should be about time for her to fall head over heels for me."

Based on what I know from reading manga and light novels, since I've let her go multiple times after our battles, I should be getting my confession of love any day…

All I need now is an event where I save her life, and then my favor with her will be maxed out, I'm sure.

"F-fall for…? Um, well, she said you were a very strong person…"

I find Camille's evasiveness suspicious and ask again.

"…What else? She's been trash-talking me, hasn't she?"

"N-no, not at… Well. She did mention that you took lots of embarrassing photographs of her and that you thoroughly humiliated her by stealing her underwear before she teleported, but…"

I would've complained if her words were nothing more unsubstantiated rumors, but sadly, I remember doing all that.

"But wait, why isn't Heine the emissary? Was she so afraid of being sexually harassed by me that she sent you instead?"

"N-no, that's not it at all! Lady Heine is currently—"

As Camille begins to explain, Tillis cuts her off by sharply clapping her hands together.

"That's quite enough small talk. We have far too much to discuss to fritter away our time…"

"True. I have demands of the Demon Lord's Army as Kisaragi's head of negotiations. Though, to be more precise, they concern the mysterious facilities in your castle."

As the two schemers begin talking, Camille, with a tense expression, balls her hands into fists atop her lap.

"With regards to that matter, I have already received the Demon Lord's blessing for you to conduct whatever investigations you desire."

...Huh?

"I had expected a little more pushback, but that was rather quick, wasn't it...? For our part, we would like to discuss matters of reparations and cessation of hostilities..."

"On those subjects, the Demon Lord would like to meet directly to discuss terms. As such, if you could dispatch a representative with the authority to make decisions..."

The conversation proceeds unusually smoothly. Did Lilith's overwhelming show of force really scare them into submission?

Just then, Alice and Tillis exchange glances as though confirming something.

"Understood. Then I'll head to the castle. What about scheduling?"

At Alice's words, Camille lets out a sigh of relief.

"I apologize for the inconvenience, but we would prefer if you could come immediately..."

With that, she bows deeply once again...

4

The next day.

"Ha-ha-ha-ha-ha-ha-ha! What those soldiers said made me a bit nervous, but it seems I still retain the highest confidence of Her Highness!"

As our buggy zooms across the land, Snow is indulging in some gleeful cackling.

To think she'd been locked in the dungeon by the castle's soldiers while we were busy negotiating...

"Listen up, Six. Now is the time to make use of my information. You brought my report, yes?"

"The one saying the Demon Lord is greedy and arrogant, right? Yeah, I have it. I'm kinda skeptical now. If that was true, I don't think negotiations would've begun so smoothly..."

As I voice my suspicions in the passenger's seat, Alice, driving the buggy, addresses me in Japanese.

"<If the Demon Lord is exactly as the report says, this meeting is likely to be a trap. That's probably why Tillis is sending Snow to represent the kingdom.>"

"<...So she wanders into the Demon Lord's Castle and immediately gets killed? If that's how it is, aren't we in danger, too?>"

And for that matter, I still think it's suspicious that Heine wasn't sent as the emissary.

As for the actual emissary, Camille, she's gliding through the air in front of the buggy.

"<If it's a trap, we'll just show our rivals what happens when you mess with Kisaragi. I mean, that's why we brought Rose along. We'll wreck the place.>"

She says it so casually, but it wouldn't be out of the question for the Demon Lord to be a mutant-level fighter.

In the back seat of the buggy are Rose, looking happily at the passing landscape, and Grimm, who's soundly asleep.

Rose is obviously coming along because she has things to discuss with the Demon Lord, but I loaded Grimm into the back seat while she was sleeping because she cried when we left her behind last time.

"<I mean, sure, we can't let them underestimate us as an evil

organization, but still... Are you sure we've got enough manpower here? You've at least got an exit plan, right?>"

I glance up at Snow as she sticks her head out the sunroof and cackles. Suddenly, I'm worried about our party composition.

"<It's still possible we're walking into a trap. The one thing we know for sure is that their recent defeat at the hands of Lady Lilith has them playing defensively. The negotiations might go smoother than you expect.>"

While Lilith ordinarily contributes nothing but complications, would she be the one who gets the credit in this case?

"<Besides, in the worst-case scenario, I can always self-destruct. Just leave that to me.>"

"<Why do you always include self-destructing in your options?>"

"You two need to stop yammering in your mother tongue! We're almost close enough to see the Demon Lord's Castle! You better not mess things up!"

Redirecting my attention to Snow's remark, I see the faint outlines of an enormous, fortified castle.

The building has such a modern appearance that it makes the kingdom of Grace's royal palace look like ancient ruins. I have no doubt that it's a relic of the previous era.

A while later, as we approach the Demon Lord's castle, it's clear there's no city surrounding it.

Sitting right in the middle of the wastelands, the Demon Lord's Castle looks like an impenetrable fortress.

"B-Boss, the gate opened by itself! There's someone hiding in the shadow of the entrance! We need to watch out for an ambush!"

"Heh, Rose, chill. That's called an automatic door; it's a convenience of technology that's pretty common in our country. I doubt there's anyone here."

As I explain how automatic doors work to a frazzled Rose, Camille lands near us.

Looks like she's going to be guiding us from this point on.

Which means we'll have to park the buggy here, I guess.

As for Grimm, it'd be a hassle to wake her and explain the situation, so we're gonna leave her behind.

I mean, we brought her along this time, at least, so I don't think she's going to cry.

Just then, Camille, who has been gazing intently at our buggy, confirms everyone other than Grimm has disembarked…

"Very well, please come this way… Welcome to the Demon Lord's Castle. If you step inside, abandon all hope of making it out alive—"

"Showing your true colors, huh? Raaaaagh!"

Before Camille finishes her line, I jump her!

"No, it's a misunderstanding! That was just a line we're supposed to tell everyone who comes to the Demon Lord's Castle!"

Camille sobs her explanation as I keep her restrained. Snow, meanwhile, waves the blade of her magic sword in front of our guide.

"You have some nerve to suddenly threaten me, the kingdom's emissary…"

"Please wait! It really is an old custom! I'm not lying! Please believe me!"

While Snow refuses to hear Camille out, Alice and I each place a hand on the knight's shoulders.

"Hold on, Snow, she's probably telling the truth. It likely is the custom to greet visitors to the Demon Lord's Castle with that line."

"Six is right. I wouldn't be surprised if our competitor had their own manual full of rules and guidelines."

As Alice and I nod in understanding, Camille and Snow widen their eyes.

"Um, wow, I didn't expect humans to understand a custom that even most demons find meaningless..."

"Y-you two seriously think there's a custom that's this stupid?"

Both Snow and Camille sound thoroughly surprised, but it's common practice among evil organizations.

After all, the Kisaragi manual dictates its own method of dealing with intruders.

And of course, next to me, Rose, who is probably the most sympathetic to this sort of theatrical display, nods along.

"...I don't understand why, but it seems I'm the only one who doesn't get it... Very well, I'll let it slide this time, but try to avoid any confusing statements like that in the future."

"B-but there's a customary greeting before you meet the Demon Lord... I'm sorry, I'll skip it this time!"

With Snow still brandishing her magic sword menacingly, Camille proceeds.

I figured the Demon Lord's Castle would be filled with demons, but oddly, the castle itself seems pretty empty.

We occasionally run into some armored orcs, and Rose intimidates them each time by looking at them with the eyes of a starving predator.

Considering where we are, I was expecting much creepier decor, but the interior is well lit, and the hallways are all spotless.

Eventually, we begin climbing a seemingly endless flight of stairs. Just as my thoughts go to the fact that both Kisaragi Supreme Leaders and the Demon Lord were alike in preferring to live in high spaces—

"Now, if you could all come this way. Beyond this door awaits the Demon Lord Viper."

Our guide, Camille, stops in front of a giant door.

The Demon Lord is supposedly haughty and selfish.

But apparently, he's also committed to bringing glory and prosperity to demonkind.

Snow had been babbling something about taking the population of the demon territory hostage to get an advantage in negotiations, but...

...Wait, the Demon Lord's name is Viper?

I could've sworn it was Mailman or something.

Just then, Snow moves from her spot near the door and circles behind me.

"Well, let's allow our commander the honor of going in first. We leave it to you to make a good first impression, sir!"

"Screw that! Don't only call me Commander when it's convenient for you! What happened to all that enthusiasm you had on the way here? I don't wanna go in first, either!"

Ignoring our attempts to shove each other through first, Alice fearlessly opens the door.

Inside the middle of the dimly lit room, we can see the outline of a person.

And standing there is...

"Welcome, brave yet foolhardy humans... In acknowledgment of the courage it took for you to appear before me, I shall grant you all swift and painless deaths..."

...a beautiful, silver-haired young woman who looks nothing like the Demon Lord described in our briefings. Her face is beet-red as she delivers her address.

5

According to Snow's information, the Demon Lord was supposed to be some middle-aged guy.

So who the hell is this hottie trying to play it cool while blushing all the way to the tips of her ears?

Anyway, first things first.

"Sorry, I didn't quite catch that. From the top, please."

"Huh...?"

The bashful girl clearly wasn't expecting anyone to request an encore, and she freezes.

"Yeah, I need to hear that again. I'll record it this time, so go ahead."

"Um... A-all right, I understand... One more time, then..."

"Lady Viper, you don't need to bother with the customary greeting! These people are just teasing you, Your Majesty!"

As the trembling young woman prepares to repeat herself, Camille hurriedly stops her.

I'm sure the whole thing about a "swift and painless death" was just a part of the Demon Lord's greeting. The Kisaragi Supreme Leaders all have similar rehearsed lines, so I get it.

Standing at the head of our group, Alice speaks up.

"I'm the negotiator representing the Kisaragi Corporation, Ms. Alice. Given that we're on the top floor of the castle and you're being addressed as *Lady* Viper, can I assume *you're* the Demon Lord?"

...Huh?

"Wait, hold up. Is this girl really the Demon Lord? ...Thank god! Having some edgy old man as the Demon Lord is so overdone! She seems like a pretty normal girl if you ask me, but that's still way better than a guy!"

"You're in Her Majesty's presence! Get a hold of yourself!"

As my mood skyrockets, Camille does her best to calm me down.

"E-emissaries of the kingdom of Grace, I thank you for coming all this way. It's a pleasure to make your acquaintance. I am Viper, the Demon Lord," Viper, still blushing, introduces herself.

"...Now, then. Camille, thank you for your exemplary service thus far. I'll take it from here. In my absence, I leave things in your capable hands."

"Y-Your Majesty...! ...Please take care!"

For some reason, Camille is on the verge of tears as she says this and repeatedly turns to look at Viper while making her way out of the room.

That's weird. The information we got ahead of time mentioned a haughty, selfish personality, so what was with that exchange?

And what did she mean by "in her absence"…?

Still, I decide to do as I was instructed by Alice on the way here and intimidate the enemy.

"First off, the pleasure's all mine, Your Majesty. I'm Combat Agent Six. You can go ahead and call me Mr. Six. Feel free to think of us as mercenaries hired by the kingdom of Grace. Our organization's name is the Kisaragi Corporation. Like you, we're also an evil organization."

"A—a pleasure to meet you, Mr. Six. I have heard much about you from Heine of the Flames."

For some reason, the Demon Lord shuffles backward after learning my name.

Just how badly did Heine drag my name through the mud?

"I don't know what she said about me, but we have two demands! First, I trust you're aware of how powerful we are, judging by the results of our recent skirmish. But if you insist we keep fighting, we're happy to oblige! Just know if you are willing to agree to a cease-fire, then we demand reparations. Second, I want you to have a chat with this girl here."

Without relaxing my intimidating stance, I lightly nudge Rose from behind.

"Um, I'm Rose, a Battle Chimera! I'm here today to ask the Demon Lord about my origins!"

As Rose's voice cracks from nerves, Viper smiles gently and responds:

"Of course. I'm aware of your request, and I hope Russell, your fellow Battle Chimera, is doing well."

"Y-y-yes! He seems very happy doing chores while dressed as a maid! He complains a lot, but he does so with a smile!"

"Chores? While dressed as a maid? I see... If he's happy, then that's what is important. But...a maid? Why is he wearing girls' clothes?"

Viper seems to be struggling to come to grips with something, but now's not the time to dwell on Russell's preferences.

"Yo, Ms. Demon Lord, putting aside the cross-dressing Chimera, let's talk about the glutton Chimera instead. It looks like the weird facilities under this building are related to Rose somehow. Let's have a look at those first, shall we?"

"Oh, of course. I'll show you around, then. This way, please."

Saying that, Viper steps to the side and continues out the door.

...Huh?

"<Alice, Alice, I think she's really gonna give us a tour. What do you think? Is this a trap?>"

"<No, but I would have thought the mystery facilities would be an important bargaining chip for them...>"

As we start our discussion in Japanese, Viper tilts her head curiously at us.

If she's going to show us around, we may as well go take a look.

Still, the more I look at Viper as she leads the way, the more she just seems like a normal girl to me.

"Hey, Alice, isn't it crazy how reliable Snow's intel was? The Demon Lord's a greedy, arrogant old man, just like she said he'd be!"

"I know, right? She did say her network of information was the best of the best, but I'm truly blown away."

"Wha?! N-no, you've got it all wrong! According to my information, the Demon Lord is supposed to be a middle-aged man! Besides! The name is different! The Demon Lord's name was supposed to be Mehlmehl!"

Snow desperately lines up her excuses, but her information's already worthless.

Viper, who has been walking in front of us, stops and turns around. "Mehlmehl was my father. That is…I recently succeeded him…"

…?

"Hey, Alice, isn't a succession at this time a little weird? And this girl doesn't really seem fit to be a Demon Lord."

"…It's definitely weird. It'd be best if we could have someone give us more information."

Well sure, but the only person we know related to the Demon Lord's Army is…

Oh, right, Heine. Where the hell is she? Being able to ask her would make things a lot easier.

"Hey, Ms. Demon Lord, why isn't Heine around? What's she up to? We figured she would've been the one sent to talk to us."

At my words, Viper looks a little bit at a loss.

"…Heine is currently imprisoned in the dungeon. Would you like to see her?"

6

We follow Viper into the dungeon, where Rose makes an odd observation.

"…Huh, this place looks familiar for some reason…"

She then looks around curiously before wandering off into a random room.

"…Hey, Ms. Demon Lord, is it fine for her to just wander around like that?"

"Yes, it's not a problem. After all, wasn't her goal to investigate this area?"

Rose's sudden behavior sort of bothers me, but if Viper doesn't have a problem with it, then I guess I'll just let her do her thing.

Anyway, Heine comes first. I need to see her and ask her just what's going on…

*   *   *

I suddenly feel someone's gaze on me, so I about-face and lock eyes with a flustered Heine. She's imprisoned in a spotless jail cell.

She's sitting in the middle of the cell with her knees cradled against her chest. She freezes in place and stares at us.

I point to Heine and—

"Look at that! One of the Demon Lord's Elite Four is locked in a cell! Wow, how embarrassing! Bah-ha-ha-ha-ha-ha-ha! That's rich! Ah-ha-ha-ha!"

"S-Six, you bastard! Stop laughing! Who do you think is responsible for the situation I'm in?!"

"Ha-ha-ha-ha-ha! Good job, Six! Keep taunting her! That bitch melted one of my magic swords! You there, guard, do you have anything long and pointy? Like a stick, perhaps? I want to poke her through the bars!"

As Snow and I mock her, Heine grabs hold of the iron bars of her cell and yells back at us, but it seems her sorcerer stone has been taken from her, leaving her unable to summon her flames.

I move close enough so that I'm just out of reach from the opposite side of the bars.

"Hey now, you shouldn't blame other people for your problems. What wrong? Are you grumpy because they don't feed you anything tasty down here? Here, have everyone's favorite snack, Calorie-Z!"

"S-screw you! I don't need your charity...... You asshole! If you're gonna hand it over, then hand it over! Stop teasing me! I'll kill you!"

<<Evil Points Acquired. Evil Points Acquired.>>

As I wave the calorie bar around just out of Heine's reach, Viper places her hand on my shoulder.

"I understand you harbor hatred toward Heine for killing many of your kingdom's soldiers. However, she was only following the orders of her country. Please..."

I guess, to Viper, it looked like I was trying to get revenge for my fallen comrades.

To be honest, I just really, really like teasing Heine. However...

"Your Majesty, you're giving him too much credit! That bastard just gets off on making me miserable!!"

"...Is that so?"

At Viper's inquisitive look, I shake my head with a solemn expression.

"No, Heine has killed scores of our comrades. This is to avenge their deaths. Snow, pass me the stick. This is for the goldfish that died because I forgot to feed it! And this is for Koromaru, who ran off when his leash broke during a walk! And this is for having the mokemoke I'd befriended slaughtered right before my eyes!"

"Stop it! Stop poking me! I had nothing to do with your goldfish or your mokemoke friend! And who the hell is Koromaru?!"

<<Evil points Acquired. Evil points Acquired.>>

After poking Heine to my heart's content, I finally ask her the question that's been on my mind since I got here.

"So why are you locked up anyway?"

"That should've been the first thing you asked! I stand accused of conspiring against the country! Remember how your boss bombed the towers maintaining the barrier?! It turns out that for some reason, His Majesty, Mehlmehl, was in one of them!"

...

"Oh shit... What're we gonna do, Alice? Our useless boss did it again! The whole succession is *our fault*!"

"Calm down, Six. It's too soon to panic. First, we should check on the safety of the previous Demon Lord."

I regain my composure after hearing Alice's calm rationale.

Yes, she's right. After all, this is a Demon Lord we're talking about. He wouldn't die that easily...

"My father, the previous Demon Lord, stated he was going to

conduct maintenance on the shield before the enemy arrived, then went to one of the towers. A while later, that tower suddenly exploded, and when I arrived on the scene, I found my father's body—"

"Shit, shit, shit! We really did it this time, Alice! We killed her dad!"

"Calm down, Six. This is where we pin the blame on them instead. Heine, we'll blame it on Heine. We did check with her, after all, if there was anyone in the towers."

I follow Alice's suggestion and turn my ire on Heine.

"Hey, Heine! You swore there was no one near the towers!"

"I did! But—but…usually, those towers are off-limits to anyone but the Demon Lord, so there's almost never anyone there! And Lord Mehlmehl's 'may-te-nants' ritual only takes place about once a year! I didn't think it could… Oh, I didn't…"

Damn it all. Just when I thought Heine had done something useful, she totally fails to stick the landing.

And for that matter, what the hell, Mehlmehl? Who just takes a midnight stroll to a fortress tower?

"…Ah, wait a second! Then what about Rose? We agreed to the cease-fire because the Demon Lord was supposed to know a lot about Chimeras and the mystery labs! This means we wasted our time coming here!"

"D-don't blame me! You're the ones who killed Lord Mehlmehl! He did know a lot about Chimeras… W-we should call this a draw…"

She's got some nerve.

Still, at least I know why Heine's locked up.

"…So what happens to you now? I mean, you helped kill the Demon Lord, right? We're the enemy, so it's no skin off our noses, but in your case, that's treason of the worst kind, isn't it?"

"Wha—?! B-but I…"

Yes, we executed the bombing operation because she insisted there was no one near the towers.

Which means she's the one most at fault.

Listening to our exchange, Viper looks sorrowfully at Heine.

"Ordinarily, execution would be unavoidable, but given Heine's long service as one of the Elite Four, her punishment might be reduced to enslavement if she's lucky..."

"E-execution or enslavement...? Oh no, no, no..."

Based on Heine's cry of despair, enslavement must be a punishment nearly as undesirable as death.

That reminds me. Even though we lost our primary lead regarding info about Rose's past, we still have other demands.

I've also been hounding Heine for a while now. Maybe I should offer her a little mercy...

"Hey, Alice, in addition to getting information on Rose's origins, we had another demand for them, didn't we?"

"About paying us reparations for peace... Yeah, fine, do what you want."

After checking with Alice, it seems she's caught my drift.

"Ms. Demon Lord, Ms. Demon Lord, give Heine to us. In exchange, we'll give you a discount on the reparations."

"HUH?!"

Heine lets out a cry of surprise at the proposal.

She definitely wasn't expecting me, her enemy, to bail her out.

Yesterday's enemy can be today's friend. Besides, I'm not about to let such perfect boobs go to waste.

Alice looks over Heine as though sizing her up and nods a few times.

"Yes, let's go with Six's proposal. I don't know what enslavement entails, but if you have no need for her, give her to us. We'll work her to the bone and pay her next to nothing."

"That's precisely what enslavement is! Please rethink this, Your Majesty! I can still serve!"

In spite of my gallant attempt to save her, Heine looks tearfully at Viper.

Viper strokes her chin in thought.

"...Very well, we will relinquish Heine to you."

"Your Majestyyyyy!"

As Heine grabs the bars of her jail cell and sobs, Snow points and laughs.

"Ha-ha-ha-ha-ha-ha-ha-ha-ha-ha! How fitting, Heine of the Flames! A member of the Demon Lord's Elite Four falling to the position of a slave! That more than makes up for all that you've done to me thus far! And now you're going to be Six's slave! I have no doubt that your life is going to be miserable!"

That's a hell of a thing to say.

"Stop making it sound like I'm going to do something awful to her. I mean, if things continue along this route, Heine might be executed or forced to do pervy things for her former subordinates! If anything, she should be thanking me for helping her!"

"Oh, no, those sentenced to enslavement become vassals of the country and are therefore valuable public property, so they're usually safe from harm..."

At Viper's interjection, Heine nods intently and turns to the nearby jailor.

"That's right! You might have intended to help me, but you've probably just made things worse! Besides, my subordinates respect me, so they wouldn't make me do pervy things! Right? You wouldn't do that to me, would you?"

The orc guard pauses a moment to consider before saying:

"Huh? Uh, yeah! Yes, of course! ...Um, is having you wash my back considered pervy? I mean! You wouldn't have to be naked to do that! I'd be the only one fully naked..."

"Y-you..."

As Heine recoils, Viper bows her head to me.

"Mr. Six, please take care of Heine. She's quite capable. I have no doubt that she'll be very useful to the kingdom of Grace."

"Y-Your Majesty?! I—I would prefer to be enslaved in this country!"

At Heine's half sobbed appeal, Viper smiles a thin, sad smile and murmurs an apology.

"I said you would be enslaved 'if you're lucky.' If you're court-martialed, the chances of you being executed are much higher. I won't leave you to suffer alone, however. I shall enter Mr. Six's service alongside you."

"Y-Your Majesty?!"

Heine grabs the bars in shock at Viper's surprise revelation.

"What are you thinking, Your Majesty?! Please don't do anything foolish. Surely, you recall just how dangerous and cruel this man is from my warnings!"

Well, that's some nerve considering I'm standing right here.

But I wonder what the Demon Lord joining our side even means.

"This is because you warned me about him so extensively. If I, the Demon Lord, go to face my fate at the hands of a man like that, no doubt the humans victimized by the war will feel some satisfaction."

Y'know, describing time with me as an awful punishment hurts my feelings a little...

"You two seem to have some interesting ideas about me. Since you're so insistent, I might as well indulge those thoughts of yours..."

"Oh! N-no, you're wrong! I do think you're a good guy deep down! You tried to save me from being executed, after all! I really do appreciate it! H-honest!"

Heine seems to have finally figured out her situation, but it's way too late.

She'll have to content herself with becoming a good source of Evil Points...!

"Very well. You may do whatever you wish with me."

"Your Majesty!"

Viper's commitment causes Heine let out a cry of despair.

"...So, uh, this means you'll be accepting the cease-fire, right? And that you'll be coming over as hostages for the duration?"

I mean, even I'm not gonna do terrible things to hostages.

If anything, having her say this stuff so bluntly makes it hard to...

"No, we're not accepting a cease-fire."

...Huh?

"The Demon Lord's Army no longer has the strength to fight. Now that we've lost the previous Demon Lord and most of the Elite Four, if the war persists, it will spell the slow and agonizing end of all demonkind. For that reason, the Demon Lord's Army hereby offers its unconditional surrender to the kingdom of Grace and the Kisaragi Corporation. And then..."

After saying all that in a single breath, Viper pauses to gather herself...

"...and then, once all is said and done, I would like you to execute me in the Grace Kingdom."

She said this with a resolute gaze. Her expression contained all the grace and authority of a true Demon Lord.

[Status Report]

Dear Supreme Leaders,

When last we spoke, we saw over the monitor that Lady Lilith was all tied up. How's she doing now?

Without further ado, I'll give my report on our current situation.

So......the Demon Lord's dead.

It looks like he was caught up in the bombing operation executed by Lady Lilith.

Thanks to that, our investigations into our new agent Rose's origins have hit a dead end.

A member of the enemy leadership, Heine of the Flames, has been made a slave for her part in the incident.

The Demon Lord, who ordinarily would have died in an epic battle with the Chosen One, ended up getting killed off-screen by a bombardment Lady Lilith fired while picking her nose.

The situation is now much more complicated thanks to her, so please make sure her punishment is thorough.

With the situation as it is, I won't be coming back to Earth for a while longer.

—P.S. I would like to extend my thanks to Lady Lilith for effectively increasing the number of women working with me.

Reporting Agent:

Combat Agent Six

CHAPTER 2

It's Usually the Boss's Fault

1

We're finally back at the base.

I take Heine, who's been loafing around, out to the construction site for our future city.

"…I don't know how else to say this, but you people really are several kinds of ridiculous…"

Seeing the Combat Agents busy themselves with work on infrastructure and buildings, Heine's been in a state of mild shock ever since.

Thanks to the special materials, which are light, durable, and fireproof, the buildings are going up at a steady rate.

The various types of construction equipment scared her at first, but when she saw the countless pieces of heavy machinery working to move building materials, Heine could only stare with her mouth agape.

The Combat Agents looked smug upon witnessing Heine's expression.

Yeah, I get it. This is the sort of reaction I've been dying to see, too.

Using Earth's modern devices to completely redefine a primitive planet's idea of technology.

That's what I really wanted to use my Evil Points for.

My original plan was to be an exemplary Combat Agent and use them to summon some crazy-advanced weapons in the heat of battle, but I'd say blowing the locals' minds with high-tech construction equipment is a close second.

"This is our true power. You guys are lucky the war ended before I showed off what I'm *really* capable of..."

Hearing me wax sentimental, Heine lets out a note of surprise.

"When we first met, it looked like you were struggling..."

"Okay, next, I'll take you to the residential district. You really are in luck, having me, the boss, show you around. There's nothing wrong with getting in my good graces while you can."

After I completely ignore her comment, Heine shoots me a skeptical look.

"S-so should the boss really be spending all his time giving me a tour, then? Aren't you busy? I don't particularly mind if someone else..."

"Don't be stupid. Look at the lascivious stares those men are directing your way. Think about the situation you're in. They're not bothering you because you're tagging along with me, the strongest and most important one here. I'm doing you a favor!"

Overhearing our conversation, the working Combat Agents shoot me nasty glares.

"The hell, man?! Don't fill the rookie's head with lies!"

"You're being put on guide duty because you can't operate heavy machinery for shit! Besides, *Alice* is in charge around here, and Tiger Man is the strongest agent!"

The foulmouthed Combat Agents all pause their tasks just to yell at me.

"Considering the only thing you're good for is fighting, you're in no position to talk shit!"

"Oh, shut up! Who cares about a bunch of third-rate losers with double-digit designations?! I've served longer than all of you, so you damn well better respect me! Besides, I'm smarter than the lot of you combined, you dumbasses!"

With that, the lackeys' expressions turn dark.

And then—

"Hey, looks like Six is hungry for an ass-kicking! He's filling his squad with women like he's trying to put together a harem or something!"

"All you're good for is being Lady Astaroth's arm candy! How about you get your ass back to Earth and suck up to the Supreme Leaders some more, huh?!"

"Useless asshole! Don't act like you're some big-shot senior agent just because you've been around a little longer!"

The bottom-feeders step away their heavy machinery, faces red with anger like they're ready to pounce.

I crack my knuckles and get ready to show them why I'm the top dog around here.

"Oh yeah? Bring it on, chumps! I'll knock some sense into all of ya!"

"Hey, stop that! Aren't you guys supposed to be on the same side?! How can you go from friendly to fighting in the blink of an eye? You're even more bloodthirsty than demons!"

Having shown the rank-and-file Combat Agents who's boss, I've escorted Heine over to the residential district.

"Hey, are you sure you're okay…? They really did a number on you…"

"Meh, that sort of thing is just part of our daily routine. Also, saying they did a number on me makes it sound like I lost, so please phrase it differently."

My recovery enhancements will have me healed up in no time, meaning their attacks didn't do any lasting damage. So if you ask me, I didn't lose.

But Heine looks shocked by my words and stares at me.

"They were taking turns beating on you, and I'm pretty sure I heard you apologizing. I don't think you can spin that into anything other than a loss…"

"Nah, I was just pretending to surrender. Like a tactical retreat or whatever. So long as I make sure to hunt them down and ambush them one by one later, I'll still be the winner."

For some reason, Heine shrinks away after hearing my brilliant plan.

I then lead the troubled Heine to the dorms built in the residential district, open the door, and—

"This is where you'll be living… Oh hey, it's the Demon Lord."

—on the first floor of the dorms, we run into Viper buried in paperwork in the corner of the lobby.

2

Previously, at the Demon Lord's Castle's underground facilities.

Hearing Viper's request to be executed, Heine drops her gaze inside her cell.

"Um… What're you talking about? Aren't you technically the Demon Lord right now? You're a really important person. I'm pretty sure the demons are gonna be in a bind if you suddenly kick the bucket."

Seeing I'm clearly not a fan of her death wish, Viper gives me a gentle smile as if to reassure me that she's not simply being self-destructive.

"I have already ordered Camille, my lady-in-waiting, to take the demons to the allied kingdom of Toris. Our alliance negotiations had included terms of that sort… However, in the event that they're denied entry by Toris, I do have one request."

Viper, looking every bit the ruler, fixes her gaze on me.

"I'm told by our scouts that you're currently settling the Cursed Forest and building a city there. Perhaps you could use laborers? I know it's presumptuous of me to ask, but the soil in the demon territory can no longer grow crops, and we're now out of water. If you can guarantee them the minimum amount of safety, I have no doubt they'll be happy to live and work in your city."

Alice and I exchange looks at the unexpected proposal.

"<What do we do, Alice? She's offering to give us the residents of her country. But isn't the whole point of invading and settling this planet to make room for people from Earth to live here?>"

"<We won't be migrating anyone from Earth until we've done more surveying. We haven't researched yet all the planet's viruses. It would be less than ideal if we moved people here only to have them die from some mystery ailment... Still, we should be the most hated enemy for the Demon Lord's Army. We killed their previous Demon Lord, after all. I'm not sure why they'd even wanna come work for us.>"

Viper probably realized we're using our own language to communicate after listening to several of our conversations in Japanese.

She shows no sign of unease, waiting with a serious expression until our discussion is over.

"I gotta ask you something, Ms. Demon Lord. Why us instead of the kingdom of Grace? I mean, we're the ones who...you know...offed the last Demon Lord. And we're an evil organization, so..."

"Concerning my father, I don't believe it was a matter in which you had any choice. After all, we were the ones who started the invasion, so we have no right to complain. As for why I'd like my people to be settled in your city, Mr. Six, well... I've heard beastfolk are treated quite well in your organization. Orcs are treated as livestock in Grace, so I believe your city would be a better choice..."

Beastfolk? What's she talking about? I don't think Rose counts as "beastfolk" or whatever.

...Oh! I guess she means people like Tiger Man!

Well, I suppose he looks closer to a demon than a human, but he's just a mutant who was made through surgical enhancement. He's *technically* not a beast man.

"...What do you think, Alice? Sounds like a pretty sweet deal to me."

I mean, I've heard there are quite a few attractive races among the demons like succubi and vampires.

Yep, I remember what Heine said way back when.

I haven't forgotten what she offered me that time she tried to recruit me into the Demon Lord's Army.

"No objections on my part. We're short on labor at the moment. Besides, we came here to negotiate at an advantage. An unconditional surrender is way better than we bargained for. That just leaves the question of reparations for the Grace Kingdom..."

Viper looks a bit reassured at the exchange between Alice and me.

"I'm afraid this castle now only has a small quantity of treasure, as well as the mystery facilities. I'm quite certain that's not enough to serve as reparations. Instead, as Demon Lord, I'll offer my life and body as recompense."

Well, her life is one thing, but her body...

Wait, no, that's not the important thing right now.

"As mentioned earlier, my public execution will no doubt help quell the rage of the victims. Of course, I understand it's not enough. As for the rest, it may be depleted, but they may have the entirety of the demon territory. So please... Can you please save my people...?"

She looks straight at us with an expression prepared to face even death.

Oh no, she's serious.

I've gotten so used to dealing with unserious people on a daily basis that I can't help but be put on the back foot dealing with someone this sincere.

I mean, Snow's gone quiet, intimidated by Viper's commitment.

As for Rose... Dammit, I don't know what the hell she's thinking, but she's taking a nap in the room she wandered into.

Why the hell is she sleeping in enemy territory? I don't understand what's going on!

And just as I start to panic…

…Heine raises her voice from inside her cell in Viper's defense.

"Okay, I get it! If that's not enough, you can do whatever you want with me, too! So please…"

"Well said! Given how many times we've fought, I just don't feel that guilty about doing things to you for some reason, Heine."

Right as I give an immediate answer to Heine's exclamation, I see the color drain from her face.

"H-hang on, Six. I mean, we've known each other a while… C'mon, you know I had to say that as a member of the Elite Four. It'd be a problem otherwise…"

…Just then, Alice starts nodding intently and speaks up.

"As expected of the boss of an industry rival. Self-destructing is one of evil's most coveted exit strategies, after all. Well said."

Alice is bubbling with glee. Why is she impressed by Viper's statement? And, um, I don't think this is quite the same as self-destructing.

"For now, we'll figure out what to do with you after we take you back to our hideout. We'll take temporary custody of you and Heine. Leave the negotiations with the kingdom of Grace to me. If you're moving to our city, at the very least, I'll guarantee the lives of your people."

Hearing Alice's confident statement, Viper lets out a sigh of relief.

She looks as though a great weight has just been lifted off her shoulders.

Alice spends a while studying Viper's reaction.

"…And welcome to the Kisaragi Corporation. It might be a short stint, but try to enjoy yourself. We're always happy to add a high-level evildoer like a Demon Lord to our ranks."

With that, she smiles cheerfully at Viper.

3

After yesterday's exchange, we returned to the buggy, where Grimm, seemingly incapable of unlocking a car door, was tearfully pounding on the windows.

We got back to the hideout with Grimm complaining all the way, first about waking up in some random place, then about the fact that there's more women all of a sudden, but anyway—

"Hey, Demon Lord, what are you up to this morning?"

As I approach her with Heine in tow, Viper looks up from her pile of paperwork.

"Good morning, Mr. Six. When I asked Ms. Alice if there was anything I could do while waiting to learn my fate, she gave me all this..."

...Wait, so she voluntarily looked for work because she had nothing to do?

We're currently discussing Viper's fate with the kingdom of Grace.

For the kingdom's part, they can't just pin all the blame on the deceased previous Demon Lord and let bygones be bygones.

In the worst-case scenario, they might just demand Viper's life as payment. I don't really think she needs to be looking for work to do under these circumstances, but I guess she's a diligent girl at heart.

I glance over at the stack of papers to see what she's doing, but because they're in this planet's language, I can't make heads or tails of it.

"What're you working on?"

"Oh, this concerns the allocation of materials to the construction site and where to assign laborers, along with the schedule and—"

I hold up a hand and cut off Viper mid-sentence.

"I got it. If there's something you don't understand, make sure you ask for help."

I say this with the air of a dependable superior, and in response, Viper picks up a sheet from the stack.

"Oh... In that case, I wanted to ask about this subject..."

"Sorry, Demon Lord, I'm a little busy right now. Ask someone else."

"Y-you're such a..."

...As Heine directs an exasperated gaze in my direction, Viper, having put the document back, asks a bit shyly:

"Um... Mr. Six, since I've surrendered to the Grace Kingdom, I'm no longer the Demon Lord. So...if you could please call me by my name..."

Viper then looks up at me, but I can't help but notice Heine glaring daggers at me.

"You do know she's my leader as well as the former Demon Lord, right? Don't you dare disrespect her...," says Heine in a threatening whisper. I guess embarrassing nicknames are out...

"All right, then 'Vi' it is!"

"That's it, I'm kicking your ass!"

While Heine breathes fire, for her part, Viper smiles gently as though to say she doesn't mind.

"Lady Viper, you may be a prisoner, but you're still allowed to get mad, you know. If you don't, he'll just keep trying to push his luck."

"I truly don't mind how I'm addressed. But let's move on for now. Heine, have you been given a job?"

In sharp contrast to the short-tempered Heine, Viper smiles rather serenely.

"So, Vi, the thing is...Alice had her try a whole bunch of stuff, but it turns out all she's good at is fighting..."

"H-hey...! It's not like you can do anything other than fight, either! L-let me explain, Lady Viper. I tried to help with the construction, but their tools are weird and..."

As Heine desperately tries to explain...

...Squeak...squeak... The sounds of a moving wheelchair filter into the room.

Eventually, the front door to the dorms cracks open, and a pair of eyes eerily peer in...

What is this, a horror movie?

"Hey, Grimm, come in already. You're creeping me out. If you stay over there, I'm gonna throw salt and try to exorcise you."

Suddenly, the door flies open to reveal a cranky-looking Grimm. I guess she really didn't want salt in her eyes.

"...You seem to be enjoying yourself, hanging out with a former enemy and some girl you met just yesterday. *Sigh*, Commander, you're always so forgiving when it comes to women..."

Grimm's being her usual needy self, wheeling herself near Heine and shooting her a venomous grin.

"It's been a while, Heine of the Flames, pillar of the Demon Lord's Elite Four. To think that you, our former foe, would end up as the commander's concubine..."

"Now wait just a minute! You take that back..."

A vein on Heine's forehead twitches at the comment, and Grimm backs away, clearly intimidated.

...But the moment she notices Heine isn't in possession of a sorcerer stone, she takes an aggressive stance.

"Oh, hush. With your abilities stripped away, you're nothing to be afraid of! I can't believe you took advantage of the fact that I was stuck inside the buggy to seduce the commander! Have some shame, you home-wrecker!"

"I honestly didn't expect anyone to call me a home-wrecker...! I didn't seduce him or steal him away! I was forced into being his slave!"

Ignoring the dramatization of Angry Wife versus Jealous Mistress, I call over to Viper.

"Vi, Vi, it's loud in here with those two arguing! Let's go play outside."

"Huh...? B-but...I have a lot of paperwork to do..."

Ordinarily, she shouldn't have to do anything until a decision has been made regarding her fate, but I guess she's conscientious to a fault. She's oddly reluctant to abandon her work.

"Hold on! Commander, I just heard you call her Vi! When did you two get so close?!"

"I agree with this gloomy curse-woman! Stop calling her Vi!"

As Viper responds with a forced smile, Grimm puffs out her cheeks.

"I mean, I've known you longer! I deserve a pet name, too!"

"...Okay, that's asking for too much. You're a little too old for that."

Grimm takes out a doll and readies a curse, so I grab Heine and hold her in front of me as a shield.

"Hey, quit it! If you're going to bicker, do it outside! Why do I have to get dragged into this?!"

The fact that I grab Heine tighter to keep her from escaping sends Grimm into an absolute frenzy.

"How dare you flirt in front of me, you home-wrecker!"

"How the hell does this register as flirting to you?! Is something wrong with your head?!"

Just then.

"Um, Ms. Grimm...was it? I apologize on Heine's behalf. If you're going to curse someone, please curse me. I'll endure any curse intended for her."

"Er..."

Ever the martyr, Viper steps in front of Heine to shield her.

Grimm lets out a yelp of surprise, while Viper deeply bows her head.

"I understand. You need not explain your motives. I know you have reasons to hate Heine for killing many of the Grace Kingdom's soldiers. That is why you've been picking a fight with her, is it not? Please use me to take your revenge for the fallen."

"Lady Viper, I doubt this witch is thinking that deeply about this. Her reasons aren't that noble."

Viper's earnest plea succeeds in making Grimm uncomfortable.

"Commander, isn't this girl the Demon Lord? This is starting to make me feel like the bad one."

"Since you're the one picking fights at random, I'm pretty sure that does make you the bad one."

Shocked by my statement, Grimm takes a moment to collect herself before giving Viper a warm smile.

"I did come here to pay you back for all my comrades who fell on the battlefield, but I'm over that now. Rankis, who always seemed to stare intently at me as I napped in the middle of the training grounds… Oz, who seemed to have a thing for me and would always kindly push my wheelchair away, telling me I was getting in the way of training… Jed, who eagerly pounced on our fateful meeting by accidentally stepping on a handkerchief I'd dropped and then came sobbing to me begging not to be cursed and promising he would wash it… Heh, the men who I could have had futures with all died before me…"

"Y-you have my sincere…"

"Look, you gotta stop claiming any man who looks your way is interested in you. It's becoming a problem. Just think about how embarrassing it is for me walking next to you."

After I interrupt Viper's attempt to apologize for Grimm's monologue, Heine chimes in.

"So, um, is everyone in your squad like this? I took you guys pretty seriously when we fought. This just makes me feel stupid for considering you my rival…"

H-hey, at the very least, I was taking the fighting seriously, too…!

The clock strikes ten AM.

Grimm declared she was going to nap until evening, and Heine and I sat watching over Viper as she did paperwork. A short while later, Alice wandered in carrying a big stack of papers.

"...Here's some more work for you, Viper. And what're you two up to?"

"As the head of this hideout, I've been keeping an eye on Vi."

"I'm making sure Six doesn't do anything weird to Lady Viper."

"So you were getting in her way. Look, unlike you two, Viper is good at her job. Here, you can have the game console Lady Lilith left behind. Go play with it over there, Six."

I take the handheld console from Alice and plop down on a sofa.

"Ha, getting yelled at by a brat! If you want to avoid that in the future, stop bugging Lady Viper! Unlike you and I, Lady Viper's received the highest-quality education to be worthy of the throne. Which is why she's perfectly capable of governing a city!"

Heine puffs out her chest as though Viper's accomplishments are her own, and Alice retorts:

"Don't think you're not part of the problem, either. Now come with me. I've figured out your new workplace."

Heine insults me as she looks back and forth between Viper and me.

"Huh?! W-wait, I want to be with Lady Viper...! It's really risky to leave her alone with this bastard!"

"I'm a proper gentleman. I have enough restraint to delicately toe the line with people who really want me to leave them alone."

"The whole point is that you shouldn't be doing anything at all! So, Alice, what's my job going to be? Is helping Lady Viper not good enough?!"

Reluctant to leave us, Heine keeps the complaints coming.

"Oh, relax. You'll be working in a comfortable, welcoming environment and doing important work that makes use of your talents."

"What do you mean, my 'talents'?! Are you going to make me do perverted things similar to what Six is constantly subjecting me to?!"

Am I cursed to wind up in those situations whenever I run into you guys?!"

As Heine whines with tears in her eyes, I grow increasingly curious about where she's going to be assigned.

"Well, if you'd prefer that sort of work, I guess we can make that happen. But our Combat Agents are all talk and no action. They don't have the balls to follow through on anything they say to the women they harass. Besides, in our company, we may be lenient with untoward advances to a certain extent, but actual sexual assault is subject to punishment."

"R-really?! You're serious?! I can really trust you, right?"

As if gaining a measure of hope from Alice's words, Heine asks for confirmation again and again.

This is Alice we're talking about. I'm almost positive she found a better use for Heine than base perversions.

As the loud one is led away by Alice, the only sound left in the dorm lobby is that of Viper turning pages and running her pen over paper.

I turn on the game console so I can focus on that instead of interrupting Viper's work.

"No, you've already gone down this hallway! It's a dead end! Oh, oh, there's a monster following you from behind!"

"But this is the only hallway left! You sure there wasn't a puzzle on the way here?! Dammit, the monster's in the way!"

The game Lilith had been playing is pretty hard, and because I've died so many times, it didn't take long for me to ask Viper for help...

"Mr. Six, I caught a glimpse of a red button next to one of the torches!"

Peering into the small screen from next to me, Viper points at the torch in question.

"Oh, you're right! Good work, Vi! ...Dammit...! Hey, that killed me! This was a switch to a trap door! What now, Vi, what now?!"

"S-s-sorry, I'm so sorry! That's my fault; I'll take full responsibility!"

Vi's expression takes on a look of extreme concern over the fact that I died in a game.

"Don't be ridiculous, Vi. We only got this far because we worked together. I won't force you to take responsibility for a little mistake like this..."

"Mr. Six... Yes, you're right! Let's focus on getting past this point for now!"

During our exchange, the main character respawns, depleting one of his lives in the process.

Viper and I start over, determined to get through this section...

"...Hey, I hate to interrupt you two while you seem to be having so much fun, but once you've made a little more progress, I need you to get back to work."

Here comes Alice's voice, sounding as annoyed as ever.

I don't know when she sneaked in, but the android's back with a brand-new stack of papers.

".......Er!"

Viper suddenly turns beet-red and covers her face with both hands. I guess she's embarrassed for getting too absorbed in the game.

"Vi, you can't pretend nothing happened just by hiding your face, Vi. So let's just get through this level, Vi."

Despite the fact that we're pretty close to getting past this level, she no longer says a peep and isn't much help anymore.

Guess I'll have to finish this on my own!

4

It's been several days since Heine and Viper arrived at the hideout.

Seems Viper's really good at crunching through paperwork, to the point where Alice has given her an office, and she's busy at work there today.

"Vi, I've got a puzzle here. 'A fire above, a flood below. Speak my name, and thou shalt pass.' What do you think that means?"

As for me, I'm sprawled out on the couch, struggling to figure out a riddle in a game.

I really did attempt to clear it on my own, but it's important to know when to accept your limitations and cut your losses.

Scratching her pen across the paperwork, Viper raises her gaze after a moment.

"Perhaps it's the Flaming Sea Monster, the Balubalu Hydra, that's said to live on an island nation to the far west. It's a giant monster that has a brightly burning crest, and I'm told that, in order to keep its body temperature in check, it's always got its lower body soaking in the ocean."

"You sure are smart, Vi."

In the game's text box, I enter *Flaming Sea Monster Balubalu Hydra*.

"God's wrath upon the fool who answered incorrectly!"

Inside the game screen, accompanied by those words, a horde of monsters attack the main character.

"Vi! Vi!"

"My apologies! It seems I was wrong! Then the alternative is the Inferno-Frost Divinity, Magmarion. It's a demigod worshipped by a certain tribe, said to manipulate burning magma and freeze everything it touches with its frost breath."

As I input the answer as told, the screen fills with monsters.

"To the fool who answered incorrectly multiple times, begone!"

"Looks like that's wrong, too, Vi!"

The main character becomes monster food, and I'm shown the game over screen.

"My apologies! I'm sorry, very sorry! I'll pay for this with my body…"

"You need to stop offering your body at the drop of a hat, Vi! I'm a guy, y'know! It's getting harder and harder to resist!"

Just then.

A knock on the office door, followed by Rose making an appearance.

"Boss, you here? Ms. Alice told me to come play with you just in case you were bugging Ms. Viper."

"Oh? I'm not bugging her. I'm just having her help with the puzzles that sometimes show up in this game."

"I think that counts as bugging."

As Rose hops onto the open spot on my couch, she starts munching on the snacks in the office.

It's the moment Alice's plans fail and the number of useless anchors in the room doubles.

"Aren't you supposed to be here to play with me? Why are you munching on snacks, then?"

"I don't understand the reason, but I find being in the same room with Ms. Viper really soothing. It's like it helps me relax and calms me down enough make me sleepy."

It's not really a reason to toss aside her work and start eating snacks, but now that I think of it, she was napping in the Demon Lord's Castle, too.

From what I hear, the room Rose was napping in was the same one where the last Demon Lord often lost himself in his research.

I wonder if that means she's got some sort of connection to demons of the Demon Lord bloodline…

"Why are you staring so intently at my face, Boss? I'm not giving you any of these snacks. Ms. Alice is strict in limiting me to one bag a day."

Nah, I can't imagine this airheaded Chimera's got anything to do with Demon Lords.

"You know, I didn't really want any, but after hearing you say that, I wanna take 'em from you. C'mon, hand over the snacks! Resistance is futile!"

"What, are we fighting? You know I don't back down when it comes to food. Maybe it's because I've been eating lots of mokemokes in the woods lately, but I feel like I can smash rocks with my fingers when I hold them out like scissors."

After carefully placing the snacks on the couch, Rose makes scissors with her index and middle fingers, waving her hand at me threateningly.

I guess the fact that we haven't done much fighting lately means this rookie's getting a little cocky.

"You're on. It's been a while, hasn't it? Last time we fought was in the desert. I held back that time before things got too nasty, but I'm not showing any mercy this time. We're going all the way."

"Hey, I'm sorry. Let's not do this. You can have some of my snacks. I just have a really bad feeling about this... I mean, not to ask this again, but what exactly did you do to me back then?"

"I would appreciate it if you could do whatever you're talking about outside. It would let me focus on my task..."

As Viper chimes in apologetically, Rose and I agree to a truce to avoid interrupting her work any further. Instead, we sit on the couch eating snacks.

Seeing us sitting side by side and eating, Viper chuckles softly.

"When you're like that, you two look like siblings."

Rose and I exchange glances at Viper's remark.

"I'd prefer a cute, girlie little sister who regularly comes to me to get doted on."

"And I'd prefer a big brother who spoils me and gives me snacks every day."

Right as I think Rose and I are about to go at it again, I realize something.

"Hey, you've been here a while now, Vi, but I haven't heard any updates regarding the negotiations with the kingdom of Grace. They sure are taking their sweet time..."

I've left all the negotiations to Alice, but it seems she's struggling against the scheming Princess Tillis.

Rose interjects with her mouth full of food.

"Yew hafn't feard? ...*Gulp*. Princess Tillis is showing a little reluctance over the fact that we want to let demons, the longtime enemy of humankind, settle just outside the kingdom."

I guess from a Japanese-ish point of view, I feel like the decent thing to do would be to give the poor refugees a place to settle. Having been involved in this war for a while, though, I can understand Tillis's perspective, too.

This war's been going on for way too long.

Because so many men have died in battle, female soldiers are a common sight these days. That gives you some sense of just how deep the rift is between both sides.

With each nation having committed to a fight to the finish, having us suddenly show up and announce, *We're taking in the enemy, so let's play nice*, isn't going to be acceptable to most.

I mean, this kingdom's people were so desperate, they were clinging to a prophecy that a Chosen One would arise and defeat the Demon Lord.

As for the demons, with their lands turned into desert, having Lilith take out that giant lizard and open up the Great Woods for settlement is a huge stroke of luck.

But given that the Demon Lord's Army used up most of its money and can't pay much in reparations, it's hardly worth celebrating for the kingdom of Grace.

"Yeah, I can understand not wanting to suddenly be all buddy-buddy with a longtime enemy... I guess the best solution is for the Demon Lord's Army's ally nation, Toris, to let them settle there.

"I can understand why the demons had to go to war, though, given all the land they lost. I mean, I don't think I'd be able to resist, either, if there wasn't any food."

It's weirdly convincing when Rose is the one saying it, given she tried to eat me when she was hungry.

Just then—

"All Combat Agents assemble in front of the hideout. Don't forget your weapons. We're under attack by a giant monster. Get your asses out there ASAP!"

—an extremely tense announcement from Alice from the hideout's PA.

The sudden interruption causes Rose to choke on her snacks as I jump out of the office. I stop by my room to grab my R-Buzzsaw and exit the base.

5

There's a giant mole outside.

"Wh-what the hell is this…?!"

Even though I can't contain my surprise, I've actually seen this thing before.

It's the Sand King, the giant mole we ran into in the desert.

Nearby, Combat Agents have already climbed into the heavy equipment and started grappling with the Sand King.

"Ah, there you are, Six. I see you've got your R-Buzzsaw. Good, go ahead and try that. The others are using guns, but nothing seems to work on this thing."

Alice noticed me from one of the construction machines and gave me an order, but I'd rather not approach it on foot.

"Alice, get off that thing and hop in the Destroyer! The repairs are done, right?! It could handle that mole, I bet!"

"Mr. Destroyer is still having a break at the power plant. He has a voracious appetite and hasn't consumed his fill. And although he can run on either jet fuel or electricity, the former costs way too many points. Since he used up so much energy clearing away the woods, I'm recharging him right now."

But this is the sort of situation where Mr. Destroyer is the most needed!

As everyone surrounds the Sand King, it twitches its nose and stands up on its hind legs.

I always knew it was big, but seeing it looming in front of me is a wholly different experience altogether.

I'm pretty sure this thing's gonna stomp me flat if I get too close.

Just as I wilt a bit under its gaze—

"RRRROOOOOOOOOOOOOAR!"

—I hear a familiar roar echo from deep in the woods.

The great mutant Pedo Man—er, Tiger Man, one of Kisaragi's finest, is dashing this way.

The sound of his intimidating roar draws even the Sand King's attention.

Oh yeah. I remember Tiger Man mentioning something about being attacked by the Sand King last time. I wonder how he got away from this mole.

Well, we can come back to that later...

"Whoo, go get 'em, Mr. Tiger Man, sir! A mere Combat Agent like me can't hope to match a mutant in strength, so I'll provide cover fire from the corner!"

"Given that fighting's just about the only thing you do well, you'rrre coming with meow!"

Rushing into the hideout, Tiger Man lets out a loud growl to ward off the Sand King.

Is it just my imagination, or is the Sand King's attention completely focused on him?

"You ran away from it last time, right, Tiger Man? The mole seems awfully interested in you."

"I punched it with my full mewtant powerrr last time, so it's probably being cautious."

Wow, I'm impressed. That's insane.

I can't believe he ran up to a monster that big and just punched it.

"We've got a ton of people in heavy machinery this time, so let's leave it to them. It doesn't look like guns are having any effect."

I don't think I can manage something that dangerous, so I might as well make the others do the work here.

"Okay, well, you and me are gonna drrraw its attention. The moment it comes this way, the constrrruction equipment'll pin it down."

"Seriously?!"

Goddammit, I should've kept my mouth shut.

As Tiger Man and I inch toward the Sand King from the front, it suddenly starts moving its jaws.

I have a bad feeling about this, so I immediately leap to the side.

With a loud *whooshing* noise, the Sand King spits something out.

A split second after I've moved, a rock the size of a human head whizzes past the spot I'd just been occupying.

H-hold up! That was big enough to take my whole head off!

"Tiger Man, that thing's using ranged attacks!"

"Our guns don't worrrk. And as you just saw, it can attack from a distance. That've means we've got no choice but to beat it with brr-rute force."

The Sand King twitches its nose while we yell at each other.

Oh yeah, I seem to recall Alice saying something about this when we ran into the Sand King last time.

Moles are real sensitive to sound and smell because of their bad eyesight.

"Tiger Man, since I can't use Evil Points, there's something I'd like you to order."

"...Supprrression Weapon Type B? Oh, because moles have good noses. Okay, leave it to meow."

As the Sand King prepares for another ranged attack, one of the agents in the construction equipment rushes its flank.

The others take the opportunity to charge in as well.

"Six, here's the suppression weapon! My claws aren't any good for thrrrrowing, so you have to do it!"

"Whoo-hoo, take this! Graaaaah!"

I throw the suppression weapon, aka the Enhanced Tear Gas Grenade, and perfectly nail the Sand King right on the nose.

The pain of the impact and the release of the noxious gases seem unbearable, and—

"Gaaaaaah! Six, what the hell are you doing?!"

"You moron! Try to restrain it!"

"The buildings! It's gonna wreck the buildings we're working on!"

—the Sand King, reacting violently to the strong smell, throws off the construction equipment holding it down and rolls around in agony, crushing the nearby buildings.

"Those with extra Evil Points, request whaling harpoons! Fire them into that thing and anchor the lines to something heavy!"

The whaling harpoons have reinforced rope attached to one end for easy recall.

Alice senses that subjugating the target with construction equipment isn't very feasible, but it continues to howl in rage...

The Sand King then jumps into the hole it dug, before kicking up dirt behind it to seal the entrance.

6

After the Sand King vanishes, Rose and Viper come rushing out of the office.

"Are you okay, Boss? What just hit us?!"

"You're a bit late, Rose! It was a mole! That Sand King thing attacked us!"

The pair gasp at the giant hole in the residential area.

"Please excuse my lateness, Mr. Six. Ms. Rose was choking on her snacks, and she almost died..."

"Oh, don't worry about it, Vi. You're a guest. It's okay for you to stay somewhere safe... But as for *you*... You're a Combat Agent. How is it those of us who fought are unharmed, but you were having a brush with death?"

"Well, I learned something new today! Snacks dry out your mouth, so if you try to cram them all down, you can choke!"

Well, at least Rose has leveled up from total dimwit to slightly-less-of-a-dimwit. The Combat Agents who had their equipment blown back by the explosive approach me angrily.

"Hey, moron, what the hell were you thinking tossing a Type B grenade at something that big?!"

"All that talk about being a veteran, and this idiot just gets in the way."

"You listening to us, dumbass? See all those wrecked buildings? That's *your* fault! Go fix 'em!"

"Hey, lay off! Don't call someone stupid when you're plenty stupid yourself! Rose, you were late to the fight, so you better help me! Let's get this cleanup over with!"

"A-all right! I'm sorry we were late!"

After that, Rose and I get to work. Viper helps out, too, for some reason.

"What are you doing, Vi? I said Rose and I would handle this. You can go back to your room. Besides, all the bastards out here (besides me) are creeps. This really isn't the safest place for you."

""""Oh yeah?!"""""

As the creeps all fly into a rage, Viper shakes her head.

"It's quite all right. I've finished my paperwork, so please let me help. And are you sure you're all unhurt? Despite appearances, I can use some basic healing magic, so please tell me even if it's a small injury."

""""Magic!"""""

The creeps all forget their anger thanks to the promise of witnessing real magic.

"What the hell, guys? You've seen plenty of magic during your fights with the Demon Lord's Army, haven't you? ...*Sigh*, this is why having new recruits on the job is such a pain in the ass. They gawk at every little thi— Ow!"

As I'm standing there bragging about my familiarity with magic to the scumbags, one of them smacks me.

"Ms. Viper, was it? Can you please demonstrate your magic by healing this moron?"

"Oh, how convenient... You want her to heal the cheek you just smacked? You're not implying that I'm a moron and that she should fix my brain, right?"

Just as I'm picking a fight, Viper gently places her palm against my cheek and chants her spell.

"In the name of the Goddess of Time, restore thy body to good health!"

With that, my cheek, which reddened from the impact, heals as though being restored to a previous state of existence.

""""Woooooow!"""""

As the agents hoot and holler at Viper's magic, the antithetical android pays us a visit.

"That's not magic; it's just super advanced technology. You can fool these idiots, but you can't fool my crystal-lens eyes."

"You're usually dependable, but right now, your eyes are made of glass."

Alice, who still steadfastly refuses to believe in magic, says:

"Yo, Six, smack one of the Combat Agents."

"OW! Six, you son of a—! …Huh?"

As I smack the Combat Agent who hit me earlier, Alice presses her hand to his swollen cheek.

"Even knowing she's an android, it's nice to have a girl touch your cheek… Ow, ow, ow, ow! Alice, what are you doing?!"

Having held the agent in place by grabbing his face, Alice stabs his cheek with a syringe.

Shortly thereafter, the wound rapidly begins healing.

"I injected some healing nanobots. See? The power of science can do the same thing."

"Don't make me a guinea pig to compete against the supernatural!"

While that agent starts a shoving match with Alice, the others ignore them and turn to Viper.

"Ms. Viper, you mentioned something about the Goddess of Time, but does that mean your healing works by reversing time? Does that mean you can fix broken things? If so, can you fix my figurine that Six broke?"

"Can you fix tech, too? If so, then please fix the game console in the rec room that Six broke after he got upset the other day…"

As the agents all make their requests, Tiger Man, who has shown no interest in magic until that moment and has been happily helping Rose, stops in his tracks.

With a deathly serious expression, he asks:

"Ms. Viper. Can you use that magic to restore my body to that of a child's?"

"I-I'm sorry… With my sorcerer stone, the most I can do is restore a small part of someone's body to how it was a short time ago…"

The request seemed to be so important to Tiger Man that he'd even forgotten to purr while saying it. And after hearing her answer, he simply muttered, "I see," and stared off into the distance.

"Sorry about all this, Vi. See what I mean about them being creeps? Don't worry about helping out here. Go back inside. You're surrounded by mindless beasts. They might try something."

At my words, the agents clench their jaws in anger, but Viper hurriedly shakes her head.

"No, actually…I had something I wanted to ask you. I heard the Sand King appeared, but does that mean you defeated the master of the Great Woods, the Forest King?"

…What was the Forest King again?

The name sounds familiar, but did we defeat something like that?

Just then, one of the agents speaks up.

"I think she's talking about the crazy-huge mechanical lizard Lady Lilith killed the other day. At least, I'm pretty sure that's what it was called."

Oh, right, the thing that was protecting the mystery facility. Yeah, I remember that.

"I see. I understand now… When you began settling the woods, I thought you had come up with a way to compete with the Forest King, but to have killed it… Oh dear, this may be an issue…"

Viper appears to be lost in thought, muttering softly to herself.

But it doesn't sound like something we can ignore.

"Um, Vi, what did that lizard have to do with anything? Should we not have killed it?"

"N-no, well, not exactly…"

Viper hesitates as though the answer is difficult to get out, but her expression says this isn't something she can avoid talking about.

"I believe the Sand King appeared here because the Forest King is dead."

*   *   *

......

"The Forest King and the Sand King have been rivals for as long as anyone can remember. They each fight for territory. Eventually, the Forest King settled in the Great Woods near the Grace Kingdom. And the Sand King made the demon territory its domain."

The agents all go silent at Viper's words.

If she's right, there's something I gotta ask her.

"So, Vi, now that the Forest King's gone, do you think that mole's gonna come back here? ...Maybe even attack the kingdom of Grace, too?"

"I-I'm afraid so..."

...Rose efficiently cleans up the debris while Tiger Man helps. He also directs an affectionate gaze her way.

The only sounds that can be heard are coming from the people helping with cleanup. Alice, who has somehow managed to restrain the agent she's been fighting, then quips:

"Yo, Six, time for a report. Make sure Lady Astaroth and Lady Belial get all the juicy details. Don't forget to put in a punishment request from everyone present."

[Status Report]

Dear Supreme Leaders,

I hope this letter finds you well.

Lady Lilith, who already caused plenty of problems while here, has retroactively done it again. Please tie her up one more time.

It's been revealed that the reason Tiger Man's unit was attacked by the giant mole, also known as the "Sand King," was because of Lady Lilith.

She killed the "Forest King," a giant lizard, without putting any serious thought into it, and now the power balance between the two great monsters has collapsed.

It appears, at this rate, there's a high probability the Sand King will also attack the kingdom of Grace.

In fact, the Sand King attacked our hideout just the other day.

Because the situation is so desperate, we've put a temporary hold on the negotiations between the demons and the kingdom. We've also paused our investigation into Rose's origins. We are now pouring all our effort into defeating the Sand King.

As such, all the Combat Agents and mutants assigned to this world request some sort of punishment upon Lady Lilith for leaving us in this situation.

—P.S. Please inform her that if she feels even a shred of guilt, she should send us more portable console games.

Reporting Agent:

Combat Agent Six

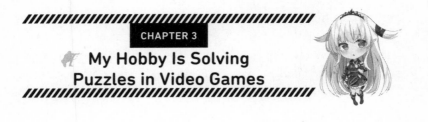

CHAPTER 3

My Hobby Is Solving Puzzles in Video Games

1

The sunset paints the area around our base in shades of gold, orange, and red.

I'm lying on the sofa in the office, playing games while Viper diligently handles some paperwork.

I've been thinking the day would end uneventfully again, but...

"...Hmm. So Alice really told you that? That you can do most of the budget allocation for the city?"

"Y-yes. Since it's a hassle for her to come up with everything from scratch, I'm to make proposals, and Ms. Alice will modify them... U-um, is there a problem...?"

There are currently four of us in Viper's office.

First, there's Viper and me, then Grimm, nitpicking through the paperwork like a mother-in-law, and for some reason, Rose is curled up and sleeping at Viper's feet.

"I don't think there's anything wrong with the overall proposal, but what about this item here? The budget allocated to childcare centers is rather high. Can you explain your reasoning for that?"

"U-um... Children are a country's greatest treasure, so I can't imagine there's anything lost by putting an emphasis on childcare and education-related items... Since this city doesn't have any settlers yet, I thought it would be important to focus on raising the next generation of citizens."

As Viper answers nervously, Grimm slams the documents onto her desk.

Viper flinches, and Grimm pokes at her with her index finger.

"Then what about households without children?! What about single women?! Taking care of children is fine, but my taxes are going toward this budget, aren't they?! Then I can't allow that! Why should I, a single woman, help support other people's children so they can have a happy little family?! I'm against it! If you're going to do that, set up a matchmaking office as well!"

Though cowed by the gloomy spinster's heartfelt statement, Viper responds:

"R-right now, there's no need for a matchmaking office in the kingdom of Grace or this city... According to Ms. Alice, once the war is officially over, the peace will bring out a wave of food and jobs, allow for a flourishing economy, and cause an unprecedented baby boom. If that's the case, it's a better use of resources to support people who already have families rather than forcing people to get married..."

"How dare yooooou!"

As Grimm throws a tearful tantrum, I come across a difficult section in my game.

"Vi, Vi, can you come here a moment? A puzzle just came up, so I need your help."

"Oh... Very well. What sort of puzzle is it?"

The game I've been playing for a while is a simple dungeon

crawler where the main character goes into a dungeon, solves numerous puzzles, defeats the dungeon master, and acquires loot.

It's mostly an action game, but the puzzles that occasionally pop up have been a real thorn in my side.

It'd be super easy if I could just ask Alice, but it feels like she'd probably read the game data, analyze its contents to start explaining the scenario, and end up spoiling it for me, so I've been avoiding going to her for help.

I mean, she's already done that to me with a different game.

Which is why I'm having the smartest person near me, aka Viper, lend me her insight.

"So there's a door in front of me, and there's a banana hanging from a rope tied to the ceiling. The only other things in the room is a stepladder and a stick. Now, thinking about it normally, it seems to be hinting I should climb the stepladder and use the stick to hit the banana, but…"

"I see. Based on the length of the stick, you won't be able to reach the banana even if you're on the stepladder… I have a few ideas. The first is that you get up on the stepladder, then jump and hit the banana with the stick. Second, this idea involves a bit more brute force, but throw the heavy-looking stepladder at the banana. Third…why not make the stick longer? Your character has a sword, yes? How about using something like a rope to tie the stick to the tip of it?"

Viper looks a little proud of herself as she proposes three potential solutions.

I see, these are the fruits of the elite education given to the Demon Lord's daughter…

"Wow, Vi, those are great ideas. I'm sure at least one of them will work."

Evidently drawn by my game console, Grimm wanders across the carpeted office floor and peers at the screen.

"That's an odd thing you're playing with… What is it? Does that door not open? Why will it open once you retrieve the banana? Why can't you just break the door down?"

Grimm proposes something off-the-wall, revealing she's totally ignorant of video games altogether.

"Why won't it open? Well, that's because of the game's overall gimmick. The door just generally opens when you figure out—"

As I try to show Grimm that the door is locked, it just opens normally.

"What are you talking about? It just opened really easily. What's the point of that banana?"

"No idea."

I mean, I really don't know what the game developers were thinking.

…Oh!

"Don't worry about it, Vi. The important thing is that it opened! And look, if the hunger gauge starts getting low, I can use your solutions to get that banana!"

Viper covers her face and turns away, seemingly embarrassed by how confidently she gave those wild proposals.

…Just then.

The base quakes, and Alice's voice comes over the loudspeaker.

"That damned mole is here again. Remember the plan I explained during our morning meetings. All Combat Agents, take your positions and don't you dare use the B-Equipment."

Since the day after the first attack, the Sand King's been randomly attacking us.

"You've readied the harpoon guns, right? All agents, fire at will!"

With those orders from Alice, the agents begin firing harpoons at the Sand King.

There's a sturdy rope attached to the back of each harpoon, and the other end is secured to an iron spike driven deep into the ground.

The plan is to use these to immobilize the Sand King and cut off its escape, then gradually chip it down.

"Take that!"

"We've got you, dammit!"

All Combat Agents other than myself are either firing harpoons from their launchers or chucking them with their enhanced strength.

Since my Evil Points are still in the red, I'm stuck guarding Alice.

"Whoo-hoo, I got 'im! Pull in the rope!"

"You're not getting away this time! Tonight, we're dining on mole soup! ...Er, wait."

A harpoon lands a direct hit on the Sand King, but rather than burying itself in its flesh, the whole thing bounces right off.

"Not again! I knew its hide could deflect bullets, but harpoons, too?! What the hell is it made of?!"

"How are we supposed to beat this thing?!"

The Sand King, annoyed by this onslaught, starts flailing wildly. The agents scream as they flee the mole's giant limbs.

Watching the scene unfold before her, Alice tilts her head and appears very unsatisfied.

"I'd received reports that gunfire doesn't work on it, but why aren't the harpoons working, either? It might be huge, but it's still a mole. I can't imagine its hide is that tough."

Harpoons might be a primitive weapon, but given that the agents have all been cybernetically enhanced, I can't understand why the projectiles they've been throwing have been so ineffective.

The harpoon guns aren't doing anything, either.

Since it's a mole, could it be that it dug deep into the ground and found some mystery metal that it absorbed into its skin?

I pick up one of the deflected harpoons off the ground.

"Release restraints!"

<Releasing power-armor safety restraints. Proceed?>

At my statement, the other agents look at me in shock.

<With restraints disengaged, the power armor will require a three-minute cooldown period for every one minute of activity. Continue?>

"Yeah, do it. This is the sort of situation where the difference in one's experience shows. A veteran Combat Agent really oughta shine here. Sheesh…"

<Releasing safety restraints. To cancel, please issue cancellation order at any point during the countdown. Ten…nine…eight…>

If the harpoon doesn't have enough power behind it to pierce the skin, then all we need to do is add more power.

Seems that simple fact doesn't occur to the weaklings who are completely dependent on guns.

"I'll show you how a real Combat Agent operates. We're assault troops who are most valuable when fighting on the front lines! Now's no time to hide in the back! Hey, you stupid mole! Get ready to meet your maker!"

As I challenge it straight on, the Sand King turns its nose toward me.

Seems it's decided from my sheer presence that I'm not an opponent it can ignore.

That, or it just likes the smell of the snacks I'd been munching on earlier.

"Yo, Six, you weren't listening to me during any of the morning meetings, were you? If the harpoons don't work, sure, release your restraints. But in that case, you're supposed to drop back for safety's sake and wait until the other agents draw its attention… You know I went to the trouble of explaining the plan every morning in case the mole showed up again, right?"

"Come to think of it, I can't remember participating in any of the morning meetings…"

…

<Power-armor restraints disengaged.>

2

"Ahhhhhh! Hurry! Please huuuuurrrry uuuupppp!"

"Goddammit, why are you always such an idiot…? Oof! Why the hell are you so heavy?!"

"He's still using the old-generation power armor?! For crying out loud, use your Evil Points and upgrade already!"

With my power armor on cooldown, rendering me unable to move, two agents carry me as the mole chases after us.

Despite releasing the restraints on my power armor, the harpoon I threw didn't do a damn thing.

"Hey, don't you think something's off here? Even the harpoon I threw with my super strength didn't work. Could it be that the mole has some sort of magical ability that prevents physical attacks? Like in a video game?"

"Leave that sort of theorizing to Alice! Just because you can't move doesn't mean you can slack off like that!"

The colleague carrying the upper half of my body yells this at me, but Alice doesn't believe in the supernatural.

"Actually, when Tiger Man punched the mole with his full strength, that seemed to have an effect. So I don't think physical attacks have *zero* effect."

The agent carrying my lower half shoots down my theory entirely.

If Tiger Man's attack worked, then it might just be a lack of power.

But given that even my throw didn't pierce its hide, using harpoons to immobilize it isn't going to work.

It's not like I'm still using the old power armor because I don't have the points to afford the new set.

Sure, this armor is inferior to the latest models in terms of agility, but it's got better strength and durability.

It also has a simpler design, and it's harder to break.

Maybe we should just have Tiger Man use his mutant strength to throw a harpoon.

…No, because of his claws, he can't really throw with much accuracy. No matter how far away from the battle the rest of us are, I bet any harpoon he tosses will find its way to us somehow.

Actually, now that I think about it, I haven't seen Tiger Man since the last mole attack…

"Oh shit, it's getting closer and closer! You guys need to move faster!"

"Pipe down, or we'll just leave you here!"

"Why don't we just leave him anyway? At this rate, it'll catch us, too!"

As expected of Combat Agents from an evil organization. They have no qualms about ditching me to save themselves.

"Please don't leave me here! If we get home safely, I'll introduce you to this girl Bianca who I met at one of the Grace taverns!"

"…Tch. Idiot. We might work for an evil organization, but we won't abandon another agent!"

"Yeah, we've known you a long time, Six! It's just dark humor! C'mon, let's do this!"

Boy, Kisaragi Combat Agents might not always see eye to eye, and they'll even make some messed-up jokes every once in a while, but they would never leave a comrade to die.

I take comfort in that knowledge and thank my lucky stars.

The two of them are doing their best, but the mole's still gaining on us.

There's a full minute left on the armor cooldown.

We might not be able to get away…

Just then, the pair, who seem to have come to the same conclusion, exchange whispers…

"Hey, I'll hold out until the last minute, but just in case…"

"Yeah, I've been through a lot with you. If we're about to be over-run, then..."

"Hey, what do you mean, 'just in case'? What are you two plotting? We're comrades, right? No, we're friends, even. Close friends who've been through hell and back together!"

The two don't meet my gaze despite my desperate pleas.

Yeah...I guess I knew what they were *really* thinking all along. That's just how Kisaragi agents are deep down.

"Well? Do you think we can keep going a little longer? Or is there no hope?"

"We should probably just get rid of—"

"You can do it! There's still plenty of distance between us and the mole! Don't give up so easily! My cooldown period's almost over!"

Just as the Sand King gets uncomfortably close and I panic at the prospect of being left behind...

"O Great Lord Zenarith, I beseech thee! Deliver disaster unto this monster! May it stumble in a spectacular fashion!"

As the curse rings out, the Sand King trips over its own feet.

Looking over in the direction of the voice, Grimm's there with Rose pushing her wheelchair.

She usually gets in the way, but she really came through in the clutch this time.

I typically mooch off her, but maybe tonight...

"Commander, my curse tripped the Sand King! Yes, MY curse! You owe me big-time for this! Enough to shave a year off that promise, perhaps...?"

As Grimm rambles on about something, I decide I can wait for next time to treat her.

<Cooldown complete. Power armor ready for use.>

The announcement comes at last, and I begin running with my own two feet.

"Oh, the cooldown's done... Hey, why are you suddenly running off on your own?"

"That bastard! How quickly he forgets that we hauled his ass all this way! The least he could do is run *behind* us!"

I hear some annoying buzzing coming from behind me, but since I reserved my strength during the cooldown period, I'm the first to get to Grimm.

"Commander, you always get in trouble the moment I take my eyes off you. I really can't leave you alone, can I? You'd be lost without me..."

After saying that, Grimm acts as though she can't help but care for me.

"You're one to talk considering you literally die every time I take my eyes off you, but thanks. Still, I'm not sure what you meant when you said I owed you."

"Even if you pretend not to understand, I'm still subtracting a year. You're keeping that promise if we're both not married nine years from now."

Grimm's yammering about something I'm still not really following, so I ignore her and turn my attention to the Sand King.

Back on its feet, the Sand King chases after one of the agents.

"Grimm, can you perform another curse? I mean, they were thinking of abandoning me, but they did help a little. I wanna make sure I don't owe them anything."

"I can, but that just means you'll owe me even more. Meaning if we're both single in eight years..."

Still ignoring her, I make a mad dash toward the Sand King.

"Boss, I'm tough, so I'll act as a diversion! Do something about it while I keep it busy!"

Rose dashes up next to me, completely eclipsing whatever the hell Grimm was talking about.

"Listen to meeeee! O Great Lord Zenarith, I beseech thee! Deliver disaster unto this monster! Have it freeze in place!"

The Sand King, chasing after the Combat Agent, stops dead in its tracks.

Having gone two for two for the first time in ages, Grimm earns surprised cheers from all the agents who witness her feat.

"See that, Commander? I'm a competent woman! So dependable! I can't guarantee I'll still be single in eight years, you know! So if you'll just sign the marriage certificate already, I'll throw in my incomparable housekeeping skills!"

Grimm's weirdly giddy after having her curses succeed twice in a row and starts rambling, and Alice throws something at me.

"Six, here's a sonic depth charge Lady Lilith left behind! The mole should be vulnerable to sound! When the Sand King opens its mouth, throw this into it! You just need to drive it away for today!"

After catching the ball Alice throws to me, I chase after Rose.

Once the two Combat Agents get far enough away from it, the Sand King's paralysis fades, and it turns its nose toward Rose, who's right in front of it.

…Just then.

"I'm in luck today! Really lucky! I feel like I can use the Zenarith Assembly's secret teachings!"

I don't know what she's planning, but Grimm stands on top of her wheelchair, carrying lots of sacrifices.

"I am a woman beyond death and destruction! The Archbishop of the Great Lord Zenarith! My name is Grimm Grimoire! Allow me to show you the true power of my curses!"

Our surroundings suddenly go dark.

It was bright and sunny up until a few seconds ago, but now clouds blanket the sky.

The agents begin looking around in confusion, clearly unnerved by the spectacle, which no normal human could produce.

Grimm listens to the confused murmurs with satisfaction, then points at the Sand King.

"By the grace of Lord Zenarith, give yourself to eternal slumber! Death is a precious gift! Surrender to its sweet embrace!"

My long-honed instincts as a Combat Agent sends up all sorts of warning signals.

Is she serious...? Even though she's usually just an annoying spinster, I guess this is what happens when an archbishop gets serious...!

"Please accept my offerings, Lord Zenarith!"

As Grimm screams to the sky, a black mist envelops the Sand King.

"Farewell, Sand King. Your name, the mere utterance of which brought whole nations to their knees as they cowered in fear, will not soon be forgotten..."

Grimm murmurs softly, then collapses into her wheelchair, a smirk dripping with confidence still on her face.

What just happened, you ask?

Well, it seems our dear Grimm just committed an especially fancy form of suicide.

The Sand King appears perplexed as well, and it keeps looking around despite the fact that the mist has dispersed.

But just then, a low voice echoes in the distance, slicing right through the air of confusion.

"Drown in a sea of hellfire...!"

Spurred on by Grimm's bravado, Rose strikes a pose and sucks in a deep breath.

I dash toward the Sand King as Rose draws its attention.

"Sleep for all eternity! Crimson Breaaaaath!"

As the mole reels back from the flames lapping at its nose, I throw the sonic depth charge into its mouth!

3

Having somehow driven off the Sand King, the general mood is now funeral-level gloomy.

"Gaaaah! We lost again! Hey, I need more beer over here!"

I gulp down a cold one in the hideout's cafeteria.

When I hold out my empty stein to the agent in front of the beer tap, he dismissively waves me off.

"It's free! Pour it yourself! Dammit, getting attacked like this over and over again is getting really old!"

We could go out to the town, but in the Kisaragi-operated cafeteria, employees can eat and drink for free, and in the evening, we get all-you-can-drink beer.

It's generally an awful place to work, but this is one of the nice perks of the job.

Since an agent's body is their most important asset, they always make sure to feed us properly, if nothing else.

"Boff, I luff Kifaragi. I get to eef fo muff effry day!"

Though her cheeks are filled to the brim, Rose is all smiles. After telling her about the employee cafeteria, she can usually be found here when she's not in Viper's office.

"You know, sometimes I envy how happy you get just from eating. When I invite Grimm here from time to time, she always says, *'I'd prefer somewhere more romantic! I don't wanna go to some cheap cafeteria or bar! And a food truck is out of the question!'* Then she throws a tantrum."

"Well, Grimm's originally from a rich merchant family. Since she comes from money, it makes sense she'd want to go somewhere nice for a date."

Despite being from money, she sometimes shows her true colors.

Speaking of said Grimm, she's currently "resting" on the altar.

According to Rose, this last death was pretty serious, and it'll take a while for her to revive.

Since she was actually pretty useful against the Sand King, her absence is going to suck, but there's nothing we can do about it.

"You know, Grimm did well today, so I wouldn't mind taking her somewhere nice. But Alice told me to stay at the hideout since we have something to do in the morning. I guess I'll drink with these losers tonight."

"Who the hell are you calling losers, asshole? You were the one getting in everyone's way, remember?"

"Hrmph! You still can't request anything because you don't have any Evil Points, but your attitude hasn't changed one bit. If you crawl around and bark like a dog, I might just be willing to let you order something that costs ten points or less!"

I punch my mouthy colleague in the face, then get on the ground and bark.

"Whoo, I can buy a new game now! I was getting sick of that shitty one anyway. Starting tomorrow, I'll finally be able to play something else."

As I happily gulp down my beer, Viper, who has been quietly eating next to me, looks up.

"...Um, you aren't going to play the usual game?"

"Hmm? Well, it kinda sucks. It's my boss's anyway. That should've been enough of a sign that I wouldn't enjoy it too much, but meh... What's wrong, Vi? Do you like that game?"

Viper seems sad when I ask her this, but in response, she only shakes her head.

"No, it's not that I liked the *game*, but—"

Just as she tries to say something...

"Well, well, well. What do we have here? A super-cute girl, by the looks. You know where you are, missy? Well, do ya?"

"Heh-heh, stop spending all your time with Six and come pour our drinks for us."

I forget what numbers they are, but the Combat Agents who saved me from the Sand King sit down next to Viper.

"Pour your drinks? But you two seem to be drinking things that don't need to be poured... Um, should I bring you something I can pour?"

As Viper stands to fetch them more alcohol instead of rejecting them or chewing them out, my colleagues start to panic.

"Oh, um, no, please don't do that, Ms. Viper! That was just our way of saying hi!"

"I'm really sorry about that. I'm fine with beer. No need to trouble yourself, Ms. Viper."

The two of them are immediately flustered by Viper's earnest response.

"Vi's a little too serious for jokes like that to work. What the hell are you guys doing here anyway? Don't turn this into a sausage fest."

As I try to shoo them away, they turn to me, faces red with anger.

"What's your problem?! Did you forget what you promised us when we saved you from the Sand King?!"

"Remember? Bianca? You said you'd introduce us to a girl you met at the bar!"

Oh, right, I did make that promise.

"Oh, sure, but I want to drink here tonight, so let's do that tomorrow."

"Really? Cool. We figured you'd complain, but you're weirdly chill today!"

"She better not come with a ton of baggage. Please don't...let her be like Grimm."

They seem suspicious at how easily I agreed.

"Nah, she's a really good girl. She's the most popular hostess at the kingdom of Grace's cross-dressing club."

I dodge their fists and drop into a fighting stance with a fork.

"What the hell are you two doing?! Have you lost your minds?!"

"Don't play dumb! Why are you acting like you don't get why we're pissed off?!"

"You're the one who's messed up in the head! 'Bianca' my ass!"

With the two of them screaming at me for no discernable reason, I try to figure out how to diffuse the situation.

"U-um, Mr. Six... That does seem a bit underhanded..."

Viper then turns to the other two.

"I can't replace Ms. Bianca, but if you don't mind, I can pour your drinks for you..."

"Wh-what should we do? What do we do?"

"I do want her to do that, but that'd make us worse than Six! ...Fine. We'll let you go this time, Six, but only because Ms. Viper's such a sweetheart."

Suddenly, they're forgiving me for some reason, but since I don't know why they were angry in the first place, I'm not happy with the outcome.

As I'm thinking of ways to get them back later, the other agents, having watched the previous scene, gather around us.

"As nice as you are, you're gonna end up being conned by some evil men. Men like us! Watch out for Six in particular. He's the kinda guy who's always adding new women to his harem."

"Oh, and in Kisaragi, sexual assault is strictly prohibited. If Six tries to do something weird to you, tell him, *I'll say you tried to rape me!* Heh-heh, if there wasn't that sort of rule, I definitely wouldn't leave you alone, heh-heh-heh-heh!"

As I'm thinking about how best to punish the minions filling Viper's head with weird ideas, she drops a bombshell.

"...? Oh, but as I've already confirmed with Mr. Six, I've made my peace with being treated that way if it means my people will be accepted as refugees..."

The room goes so silent that the only sound anyone can hear is Rose stuffing her face.

Eventually, an agent starts working their comm unit...

"I need to report this to Lady Astaroth..."

"Noooo, don't do that! It's not like that, I swear! I'm innocent! Vi's the one who came out and said that, totally unprompted!"

As I desperately try to stop my colleague from ratting me out, the others eye me suspiciously.

"Y-you're a shitty excuse for a man and a waste of oxygen, but I thought even you had lines you wouldn't cross..."

"We haven't done anything yet, I swear! I haven't even sexually harassed her because I feel like she'd just go along with anything I tried! She's a good girl! Even I pick my targets!"

"Lying bastard! You have a beautiful girl saying she'd accept anything done to her, and we're supposed to believe you just left it at that?! You always have pervy thoughts on the brain! At least a third of your time on any given day is spent thinking about that stuff!"

I might actually spend a bit more than that thinking of perverted things, but that little detail definitely doesn't help clear my name.

Turning to Viper, I try to plead my case.

"Vouch for me, Vi! I haven't done anything, right?! I haven't even verbally harassed you yet, right? Right?"

"Y-yes, Mr. Six hasn't done anything. It's true. All Mr. Six does is lie on the sofa in my office and play video games while I'm working. In fact, he often asks me to help him solve in-game puzzles. I even receive invitations to set aside my work so I can play with him..."

Despite her attempts to bail me out, Vi's not helping much.

At that moment, my colleague accomplishes his objective and looks quite pleased with himself.

"'Kay, I've sent my report to headquarters. Mission complete."

"Oh dear god, what have you done?! I've been trying to tell you! I'm innocent! I mean, I'm sorry I haven't been working that hard, but if I try to do anything, Alice accuses me of getting in the way and tells me to go play!'"

My colleagues surround Viper as if to protect her...

"Ms. Viper, has he done anything awful to you? Your outfit's missing a sleeve. Is he bullying you?"

"If it's something you can't tell us, make sure you report it to Alice. She might occasionally be useless, but she's super strict with that sort of thing."

"No, he really hasn't done anything to me...! Also, this outfit never had a sleeve there. There's a reason for that, actually..."

While Viper attempts to salvage my honor, I can't help but raise the question.

"I've always wondered about the missing sleeve. Is it just your unique sense of fashion, Vi?"

"O-oh, n-no. You see, whenever I unleash a full-strength Demon Lord Punch, the sleeve gets blasted away, so I stopped wearing one on my dominant arm."

...

The fearsome words of a Demon Lord plunge the room back into silence.

"See? I tried to tell you guys. I really haven't done anything. Demon Lords are super strong, and I don't have the balls to trying anything weird with someone like that..."

At my soft admission, my colleagues look away.

4

The next morning.

Viper and I wait for the demon refugees at the entrance to the city by the hideout.

After yesterday's commotion, the other agents were weirdly nice to me and got me all sorts of things from Earth, so I'm in a good mood today.

"You seem happy today, Mr. Six. Did something good happen?"

"I suppose you could say that, though there was some stuff that bugged me, too. It's all thanks to you, Vi."

Learning that last night's events are the cause, Viper keeps apologizing.

"I'm really sorry about what happened! It's all because I said something unnecessary..."

"Well, it's true that I don't do any work, so don't worry about it, Vi. Also, thanks to you, I was able to get lots of new games."

As I show off my newly acquired portable console, Viper seems to be at a loss.

"Congratulations. Um, even if you're playing a new game, feel free to let me know if you encounter any difficult puzzles."

With that, Viper gives a much brighter smile than when she first arrived.

"This one doesn't have any puzzles, so I'll probably be fine. Besides, playing games in the office is going to be hard since those idiots are watching me now... Oh wow, look at all the demons heading this way... Um, what's wrong, Vi?"

Even as I repeat my question to Viper, who seems a little different than usual, she just keeps shaking her head.

"It's nothing. I'm just happy that my people arrived safely..."

As Viper smiles, I convince myself it was just my imagination.

"Gotcha. Y'know, Vi, you really are a good person. How did your parents raise you? I'd like to know so I can raise my own daughter to be just like you."

"U-umm... My father always told me to be strong and ruthless and that others are there to be used, exploited—"

"Ah, I'm sorry, Vi, you don't have to answer that."

It seemed like she was about to unload a heavy tale on me, so I quickly put an end to it.

I guess Snow's report on the former Demon Lord's personality was right on the money.

Just then, the approaching group seems to have noticed Viper and me waiting by the entrance.

A young woman leading the huge crowd of nonhumans smiles widely and waves toward us.

"Lady Viper! You look well, but is this truly the case? The humans haven't done anything terrible to you, have they?"

I know this familiar-looking demon. Her name was Camille, I think.

"Yes, I'm okay. It's been a while, Camille… I assume Toris didn't accept our refugees?"

Yes, the reason Viper and I are here to greet them is because Alice mentioned a group of demons were headed our way.

Viper's words cloud Camille's smile.

"Well, um… Please look at this…"

After unfurling the scroll Camille hands to her, Viper's expression tenses.

I peer in from the side…

"Vi, what's it say?"

"'Vi'?!"

I ask since I can't read this planet's letters, but Camille lets out a huge reaction for some reason.

"To summarize, because the Demon Lord's Army surrendered, the demon territory no longer exists. Therefore, Toris is treating the alliance itself as null and void…," says Vi, looking up from the scroll.

"Meaning they don't plan to accept the refugees. But, well, Alice promised you, right? 'At the very least, I'll secure the lives of your people.' She's really good with this sort of thing, so cheer up, Vi."

"You said 'Vi' again!"

As Camille has another panic attack, Viper bows her head to me.

"...Thank you, Mr. Six, for everything... How can I ever repay you?"

"We'll need the manpower, so consider us even. Besides, Vi, you're just cleaning up your dad's mess. If you really want to make it up to me or whatever, just play video games with me. I play against my colleagues during our free time at night, but for some reason, it always ends in a fight."

"Bwaaaaaaaaaah!"

As I smile at Viper, Camille starts bawling right by my ear.

"Ugh, what the hell? Oh, it's the succubus girl. Look, we're kind of in the middle of something, so could you not interrupt us?!"

"I'm not a succubus! I'm a Lilim! And what's with YOU?! How can you call her 'Vi' so casually?!"

I guess this succubus doesn't like that I address Viper as "Vi."

"Mr. Six, I would be happy to keep you company tonight, if you'd like."

Viper herself says this with a smile, evidently not minding it.

"Company?! Lady Viper, what do you mean, 'keep him company'?! Exactly what happened with this man in the time I was away?!"

Camille appears to have completely misinterpreted our conversation, turning bright red as she peppers Viper with questions, but Viper herself, with her priority being her people, wanders off to find Alice.

"Were you not listening to my conversation with Vi? We're gonna have some fun together tonight."

"Fun?! Together?! Tonight?!"

Yeah, I'm pretty sure this girl's a succubus.

That night.

After Alice breezed through the process of assigning tents, we've

decided to treat the demons to an outdoor meal given their long jour-
ney on foot.

Currently, the one delicately doling out stew to the demons is...

"Weren't you from an evil organization? I'm pretty sure what
you're doing is the opposite of evil."

"This is all part of our invasion plan. By the way, you're a former
pillar of the Demon Lord's Elite Four, but you really seem to be enjoying serving food."

Russell, now completely at home in his maid outfit, continues
ladling stew without offering a counterargument.

"Here, eat this and get some rest. Be careful, it's hot. I know it's
got a weird, black color, but it tastes like normal stew."

"Thank you, Lord Russell. To think I'd run into you in this dis-
tant, foreign land..."

As the demons offer their thanks, Russell feigns disinterest, but he
scratches at his cheek, showing he's happier than he lets on.

While this soup line may seem like charity, doing this in a con-
quered territory substantially reduces the risk of rebellion.

People have an easy time trusting those who lend them a hand
when they're struggling.

Even if they're the enemy who caused those struggles in the first
place...

"Heh-heh, let Kisaragi's special, black stew soothe your tired
body and mind. Before you know it, you'll be working as our shock
troops..."

"Just to make sure, you haven't added anything weird to it, right?"

As Russell and I are handing out grub, I hear a soft chuckle.

Turning to its source, I see Viper standing there with a smile.

"Now, now, I won't allow anyone to mock his preferences. Not
even you, Vi. I mean, he really looks good in that outfit! So what if it's
women's clothing...?"

COMBATANTS WILL BE DISPATCHED!, VOL. 5

"Oh! I'm sorry, I wasn't giggling at that! My apologies! ...Huh, wait, hmm? Women's clothing? Wait, Russell?! Russell, is that you?!"

"...Y-you've got the wrong Chimera, Viper..."

As Viper gawks at Russell, he looks away, sweat beading on his brow.

Viper softly murmurs as she reaches for him with a trembling hand.

"Th-there can't be that many Chimeras, right? And you just called me 'Viper'..."

"...Well, that's because Six just called you 'Viper'..."

It seems he doesn't want her to see him in his current state, so Russell continues playing dumb.

"Hey, Russell, I already told Vi that you've taken up cross-dressing, and you seem to be having the time of your life. There's no need to be shy now."

"You bastard! I haven't 'taken up' anything! I'm dressed this way because it makes Tiger Man and the other agents really happy! ...Oh. W-wait... I didn't mean that the way it sounded..."

Upon hearing Russell's statement, the corners of Viper's mouth curl up into a smile.

"Oh, Russell, you don't have to lie to yourself anymore. The war is over. Please live your life however you wish..."

"Wait, Viper! You really are misunderstanding something! I don't actually like wearing these clothes, honest! Those are my true feelings!"

Viper gently pats Russell's head as he desperately pleads his case.

"It's okay. It looks really nice on you. In fact, I think you look really cute. I've always thought of you as a little brother, Russell, but I'll be sure to treat you like my little sister from now on."

"You don't get it at all! And what's up with you being called 'Vi'? I never thought I'd see the day when the Demon Lord's daughter was addressed so cutely... Oh, s-sorry, Viper, I guess it bothers you a little. I won't bring it up again!"

Russell apologizes as Viper turns beet-red and lowers her gaze.

"Vi is Vi. Sometimes, people call her Ms. Viper, but well... Anyway, Vi, why are you here?"

"...I—I—I thought I'd help...a little..."

"O-oh! Then come over here. I'll prepare helpings of stew, and you can hand them out!"

Russell thoughtfully tries to change the subject and begins ladling out bowls of stew and setting them on the table.

Viper seems a little embarrassed to be called by her nickname in front of the other demons waiting in line. Still, she does her best to hand out the meals, despite looking like she might burst into tears at a moment's notice.

She also puts a little distance between herself and us, likely so we won't see her embarrassment.

"Six, you really are an idiot. I've never seen Viper act that way."

"Now hold on, the reason Vi's acting awkward is because you were taunting her. Speaking of, what was Vi like at the Demon Lord's Castle?" I ask, sipping at a bowl of stew.

"Put simply, Viper's always been the model student. She's dedicated, smart, and kind... She's a bit shy, so she's never been good at socializing, but she's too kindhearted to ever say no to anyone. She's got a strong sense of responsibility and a tendency to always put the needs of others before her own... That's just how she is. I've never seen her laugh or cry, and she's certainly never cycled through expressions like she did just now."

"Okay, so serious question. Why was a girl like that the Demon Lord?"

Could it be she was putting on a persona as the Demon Lord's daughter? Regardless, whatever Viper was like before she came here, she hasn't changed anywhere near as much as Russell has.

The Lord of Water shrugs at my question.

"I have no idea. The last Demon Lord was really ruthless and greedy, but he had a strong sense of duty. He was pretty much what you'd expect from anyone with the title of Demon Lord. It's just baffling that a girl raised by a man like that ended up like Viper."

I guess he became the example of what she wanted to avoid.

...Oh, speaking of Demon Lords.

"Hey, do Chimeras like Demon Lords? For some reason, Rose really likes Vi. Whenever they're together, she's practically Viper's pet puppy."

"I think the puppy part has more to do with her personality, but I do believe there's some connection between Demon Lords and Chimeras. It's not like I was serving the Demon Lord without a reason. Though I'm not sure why we find them extremely soothing to be around..."

...

"Russell, you served the previous Demon Lord, right? And the previous Demon Lord was a middle-aged dude, right? Tiger Man's pretty up there in years, and a lot of Combat Agents are middle-aged dudes. And now you're saying it's soothing for you to be around a middle-aged dude..."

"H-hold up! N-no, I'm just reacting to the blood of a powerful demon! I mean, I find being near Viper soothing, too! It's not that I like middle-aged guys! ...Wait, why are you eating the stew, too?"

5

The next day.

With the arrival of the demon-territory residents, Hideout City's getting lively.

The buildings aren't finished yet, and most of the residents are living out of tents.

Food's still being distributed, and they're short on most of the little things that make life easier, but still...

"Whooooa! What's that?! It's a giant spider monster! Kill it!"

"You damn brats, don't you dare touch my beloved vehicle. I'll smack you! Also, he's not a spider monster. That's Mr. Destroyer."

Next to the recently completed generator station, Alice chases off the demon kids swarming the Destroyer.

Yep, Mr. Destroyer is popular with kids no matter the location.

"And what sort of demon are you? Your horn and tail are cute!"

"Hey, can you use a breath weapon? I can breathe acid!"

"Eek, stop! Don't pull my tail! I'm not a demon; I'm a Chimera…"

And over there, Rose, who looks more like a demon than your average demon, is being mobbed by a group of girls.

Smiles adorn the expressions of the adults as they watch those scenes unfold.

"You know, this is technically the base for an evil organization, but everyone's so cheerful…"

"M-my apologies… The demon territory was a very harsh environment, so I think everyone's just glad to be somewhere safe…"

Apparently, the lands of the demon territory are a postapocalyptic hellscape where monsters wander around right outside your door.

Although we're close to the Cursed Forest, we do have a wall protecting the city, and there's plenty of food and water.

"Man, Mr. Destroyer and Rose sure are popular. It's too bad Tiger Man isn't here. I bet the kids would love him…"

Then again, maybe it's a good thing he's not here.

He definitely wouldn't cross *that* line, but still, I wonder where he went.

"Mr. Tiger Man… He's the one who seems very strong and has really fluffy fur, yes…?"

Viper, for all her seriousness, is still a girl and seems to have an interest in animal mutants.

"Tiger Man is a real asset in the winter. He's super warm when you hug him. If we have a chance to ask for reinforcements, I'll see if we can get Panda Man from China or Koala Man from Australia to come over here. Those two are also super fluffy and are a real hit with the kids."

"I'm looking forward to it. I would really like to meet them!"

Our peaceful little conversation is interrupted by a decidedly non-peaceful android as she finishes chasing off the children.

"Tch, both human and demon brats have no manners. Yo, Six, I'm going to the castle. You're coming with me."

I won't comment on the fact that she looks like a kid herself.

I prepare to leave Hideout City next to Alice when Viper calls out to us.

"...Um, Mr. Six."

When I look over, Viper straightens up and has a serious expression on her face.

"Thank you so very much. I can't thank you enough for all you've done."

She then bows deeply to me.

"...If you're that interested in Panda Man, I can have them send over some merchandise."

"No, that's not what I'm talking about! I mean, about the fact that you're so accepting of everyone. I really didn't know how this would turn out, but you've put my fears to rest!"

With that, Viper jogs off to deter the children trying once again to climb atop the Destroyer.

...Oh, so that's what she meant.

I mean, we gain laborers, and the food that we give them is sent to us from Kisaragi HQ, so it's not a bad deal for us.

Also, there are a lot of beautiful women among the demons.

I only got a glimpse while handing out food, but there were definitely some succubi in there, too.

...Anyway.

"Well, since she's thanked us ahead of time, I'm putting the negotiations in your hands."

"Leave it to me. I'll get the best terms possible."

With the ever-dependable Alice by my side, we make our way to Tillis.

"There you are, Six. I knew you were easily swayed by a pretty face, but I didn't think you would fold *this* readily."

We're greeted rather rudely by Snow as we're shown to Tillis's chambers.

"Yeah, you're right. When the Demon Lord's Army attacked the castle, I remember being swayed by your charms when you came crying to me, telling me you'd do anything if I'd save Rose and Grimm."

"Grrr…! I do appreciate what you did back then, and I'm still very grateful from time to time! …Anyway!"

Snow blushes before leaning in and whispering.

"What the hell were you thinking? One or two of them is fine, but are you really planning to accept all the former members of the Demon Lord's Army? The people of this kingdom certainly appreciate what you did for them, but even we can't do anything about the anger over your actions this time. I mean, until just recently, our nation's mantra was *The only good demon is a dead one.* I'm sure some of our people will try to attack the city before long."

…Ah, I see. She's trying to warn us in her own way.

However…

"Remember who you're talking to. Monsters, troublemakers, assassins, and whoever else can all come at us if they want to. We'll crush 'em. We're the Kisaragi Corporation: an evil organization filled with capable Combat Agents, and fighting's what we do best."

"Well said, Six. Death to our enemies!"

"Why are you always so aggressive?! If settlers are what you need, we can do something about that on our end. So forget about letting in the demons. You're going to ruin relations with neighboring kingdoms, too."

From an average person's perspective, she's right.

And I can understand it's a bad idea for us to make enemies when we don't know a lot about this world yet. However...

"Sorry. With the exception of those who've committed crimes on our retribution list, Kisaragi's policy is to accept anyone who comes to us, no matter their history, and no matter how evil."

"Yeah, that's right, Six. If the neighboring kingdoms complain, we'll use that as an excuse to invade!"

As Snow backs away from Alice, the most bloodthirsty member of Kisaragi despite being an android, a voice calls to us from inside the room.

"Snow, that's enough. Please come inside. Let us discuss the matter in detail."

Opening the door at those words, we find the Final Boss...er, Tillis sitting confidently in the middle of the sofa.

Today, she bears no trace of her usual smile. Her anger is clear as day.

Snow, who entered the room with us, slides over to stand by her side.

"Hey, Alice, Tillis has a totally different aura today. It's hard to think of her as the same person who checked to make sure no one was around, struck a weird pose, and yelled, *'Dick Festival.'*"

"Now, hold on there, Six. Don't haphazardly reopen that wound."

"Your Highness, please stay strong! This is their attempt to put us on the back foot!"

Snow supports Tillis as she turns red and looks at the floor, her shoulders trembling.

As my Evil Point count increases for some reason, Snow glares at us in lieu of the temporarily incapacitated Tillis.

"Six, you scumbag! Everyone has moments when they want to do something foolish! Even if Her Highness handles the affairs of state, she's still a young woman; she certainly can't help it if she has an interest in a man's private parts!"

"Snow, you've done more than enough. Please see yourself out. And not another word, thank you."

Tillis's voice nearly cracks as she says this, and her shoulders tremble like crazy.

A few moments after Snow is driven out of the room, Tillis looks up with a serious expression like nothing happened.

"Six, we're going to have a serious talk, so stop teasing Tillis," says Alice.

"Fine. I mean, I don't get why she's pretending to be so professional after all that, but I'll behave."

"Sir Six, if you could please leave the room as well!"

Having been chased out of the room for whatever reason, Snow decides to pick a fight with me.

"Hmm, so they tossed you out as well? What did you do this time? Something stupid, I'm sure."

Snow's voice sounds almost hopeful, but...

"I didn't say anything weird. I did mention it was too late to pretend to be all serious, but I promised I'd behave."

"I also don't understand why I got kicked out. I was only trying to defend Her Highness's honor... But as I said earlier, Princess Tillis is a young woman of a certain age, so perhaps she's entered a rebellious phase."

If that's the case, I guess there's no helping it. That is a difficult age to deal with.

With the wall to my back, I take a seat on the floor and wait for Alice to finish negotiations.

"Still, you people really love to make your lives more difficult, don't you? Why take in the demons instead of just leaving them? What's in it for you?"

"We can't really help it. That's just how we are. I mean, the reason Kisaragi exists is because we take in everyone regardless of their past. We can't just change that because we're on a different planet."

Leaning against the wall next to me, Snow lets out a deep sigh.

She's usually argumentative, which annoys me, but for some reason, she's rather contained today.

"Do you really understand the situation? I'm a knight of this kingdom. If the negotiations between Her Highness and Alice don't go well, we could very well end up fighting each other."

Snow looks sad all of a sudden.

"...? Yeah, I guess. But it's not like your kingdom's even that strong. I mean, Grimm's probably your most dangerous citizen, and she'll be on our side next month. Plus, Rose is already a Kisaragi Recruit, so...I don't really see how we'd lose that one."

......

"Diiiiiie!"

"Whoa! What the hell?!"

I dodge the sudden attack from Snow, rolling away, and stand up.

"What's the big idea, Lady Sneak Attack?! Are you trying to kill me ahead of time just in case we end up going to war?! How deplorable! Just how many negative traits do you need to pile on before you're satisfied, you cheater?!"

At my justified criticism, Snow raises her brow in anger.

"You imbecile! You're the last person who can call anyone a cheater! If we go to war, I'll kill you first!"

"Oh yeaaaaah? There's no way you'd be able to kill me. I'm too strong! I'd just take you out the moment you tried! If we meet on the battlefield, you better push those needlessly huge tits together and say you're 'sooo sowwy.' I'll be sure to accept your surrender then!"

Hearing that, Snow brandishes her blade and dashes to close the gap between us.

She's serious. She's got murder in her eyes.

"Thinking back on it, we've had an odd relationship. I picked you up at first thinking you'd be useful, but you ended up being a spy. I drove you out, but somehow, you came back, and when it seemed like you'd help me, I ended up losing my rank and my fortune..."

"I'm not the reason you lost your status, you gold digger! But y'know, I don't mind apologizing a little right now! I might even give you a little bit of spending money!"

Despite my offer of spending money, Snow doesn't so much as twitch her brow. She doesn't drop her battle stance in the slightest.

I don't know why she's so pissed off, but she's not the sort of opponent I can hold back against.

"Dammit, guess I have no choice... You know, I really liked some parts of you... Like your boobs, and your body, and your boobs, and your face. You know what I'm capable of. If you wanna call this off, now's your last chance!"

"The worst part is that you're actually trying to convince me with that. I understand your skill. I know I'll probably lose. But even so, I fought my way up to the rank of knight captain! I may die, but at the very least, I'm taking one of your arms with me!"

You know, she was the first person I met on this planet.

I suppose there was never really a way for us—an agent of an evil organization and a knight who has nothing to offer but her body—to truly get along in the end.

Perhaps we were fated to do this from day one...

As I reflect and make my peace with what's about to happen, the door to Tillis's room opens.

*   *   *

"What are you two doing? Can't you stay quiet when we're having a serious discussion?"

At Alice's exasperated remark, Snow declares without hesitation:

"Sorry, Alice, but this is a fight that my knight's honor deman—"

"You want me to foreclose on your loans?!"

"Alice, stay out of this. I knew I'd have to settle things with her even—"

"You want me to cut off your allowance?!"

Snow and I kneel in the presence of the absolute power standing before us.

6

On our way back to the hideout.

Having neared the point of an all-out brawl, Snow and I start tattling on each other.

"You've got it all wrong, Ms. Alice. This man taunted me. I was trying to warn him for everyone's sake, and he started saying awful things to me."

"That's not it, Alice. She attacked me first. I was just trying to defend myself. Also, I didn't say anything awful. I was just talking about boobs."

Far past fed up with our squabbling, Alice finally opens her mouth.

"I don't care why you were fighting. Just make sure you patch things up by tomorrow. I've already settled things with Tillis and received permission for the demons to live in our city."

Snow looks absolutely shocked by the news, and I strike a celebratory pose.

"Ha-ha-ha! Well, how do you like that, Snow? Looks like we win this time! So much for us going to war with each other. Our Alice is super good at her job! Of course she'd avoid that outcome!"

"Grrrr…!"

As I taunt Snow, Alice shakes her head.

"There are conditions for letting the demons settle in our city. To fulfill those, I need you two to get to work."

Hearing that, Snow's expression turns gleeful.

"Bwa-ha-ha-ha-ha-ha-ha-ha! What were you just saying about a win, Six? Save it, loser. I just knew Princess Tillis wouldn't back down without a fight! So what are the terms? What sort of ridiculous conditions did she push on you?"

Ugh, Snow seems way too happy about this!

"Stop acting like you won, gray-hair! Depending on the demands, it could still be our win!"

"You lost the moment you accepted the terms proposed by our side! Diplomatic negotiations are all about forcing the opponent make concessions!"

The moment our fight is rekindled, Alice interjects:

"Wait until I'm done talking, you idiots. I did say there were conditions for letting the demons settle, and I also said I need you two to work hard."

"…………"

We fall into silence.

"The condition for letting the demons settle is to expunge the reason they invaded in the first place. You have to eliminate the Sand King. If we withdraw, the kingdom of Grace is next on the chopping block anyway. So as long as we defeat the Sand King, the demons will be free to live here, even if that means enlisting their aid in the effort."

…The land we founded our city on was granted to us by the kingdom of Grace, after all.

I understand that, from the kingdom's point of view, this land was intended for *us*, not the demons.

Still, demanding we take out the mole that's been terrorizing us for the past few days is a pretty big ask...

"...Hmph. Well, then you better not die in the process. The Sand King is an entity that even the Demon Lord's Army gave up trying to kill. This sort of task likely would have been no problem if Lady Lilith were still around, but..."

While I'm trying to figure out if Snow's words are jabs or genuine concern, Alice chimes in again.

"Were you not listening? You're a part of this, too."

"...What?"

[Status Report]

This mole is something else.

The lizard known as the Forest King that Lady Lilith killed the other day is nothing in comparison.

Guns and harpoons are totally ineffective.

Since our projectiles don't penetrate its hide, it just flees down a hole when it feels threatened. Even when we try to flush it back out with a sonic depth charge, we find ourselves at a point deficit because we spent most of them building up the city.

This being the case, I'd like to request that Lady Lilith, the cause of the mole attacks, use her points to send us more supplies.

To be specific, we'd like anti-giant-robot mines, hero-proof wire nets, and various other high-powered weaponry.

Also, a replacement for the figurine that broke when I messed around with it, and the game console for the rec room that just randomly decided to die on us.

For some reason, everyone's blaming me for breaking it. Please help.

Reporting Agent:

Lady Lilith's Loyal, Obedient Servant

Combat Agent Six

CHAPTER 4

Vs. the Sand King

1

So we've come to terms with the kingdom of Grace.

First, they will accept the territory the demons previously held as reparations and will not subjugate the former residents.

Second, the kingdom accepts the resettlement of the demons to our Hideout City.

Third, with the majority of the demon territory rendered unlivable due to the desertification, Kisaragi will eliminate the culprit: the Sand King.

Fourth, once the Sand King is eliminated, the demon territory should slowly begin to flourish once more. Following that recovery, the kingdom of Grace's war reparations will be considered paid in full.

And fifth, the leaders and soldiers of the Demon Lord's Army will join Kisaragi, while the residents will settle in Hideout City.

For now, the demons will temporarily shelter in Hideout City, and if in the unlikely event we conclude that the Sand King is unkillable, the demons will be driven out, the agreement will become null and void, and the war between the demons and the kingdom of Grace will resume.

…In short, everyone's happy ending hinges on us killing this giant mole.

So with that explanation out of the way…

Alice has briefed the other agents. She's now hosting a mole-busting meeting and gathering intel.

"It shied away when Tiger Man punched it and when Rose breathed fire at it. So one glaring truth is that we don't have enough firepower as we are. We should just get Lady Lilith to come back. Besides, she's the reason the former Demon Lord is dead *and* why the Sand King is attacking. She should take responsibility."

As the agents nod at my comment, one of them raises his hand.

"Nah, she'll probably screw up something again and end up adding to our problems. Let's ask for Lady Belial instead. If we can have her burn away the Great Woods along with the mole, it'll really move our settlement plans forward."

Y'know…he makes a good point.

While more agents start nodding in agreement, Alice throws a wrench into the plan.

"Requesting the assistance of the Supreme Leaders is a no-go. The report we recently sent resulted in more punishment for Lady Lilith. Finally fed up, she threw a fit and launched a rebellion. She's been calling on mutants and agents to join her but hasn't received any support so far, so she's holed up by herself. Since only another Supreme Leader can deal with her, we won't get any help from them until they have her under control."

It certainly sounds like something Lilith would do, but what's she trying to accomplish?

"In that case, we'll need some powerful weapons to take on the

VS. THE SAND KING   113

Sand King, but... Hey, you guys, how are you doing on Evil Points? I'm still in the red, so I can't order anything."

That said, my current point total has recovered up to about negative sixty.

At this rate, I should be able to use the transport system again in a few days.

"That mole was shrugging off rounds from an anti-materiel rifle, so it's more heavily armored than a tank. How many points would it take to get a weapon capable of damaging that?"

"I've been blowing my points on porn ever since I got here... The lack of convenience stores and rental shops really hurts..."

"Plus, over here, it costs points to get booze and cigarettes. But is the mole's hide actually that tough? Are we sure it isn't some sort of magical barrier or something?"

Everyone starts pitching their theories, but nothing useful comes of it.

We get some proposals for using nets woven out of wiring, and the idea that maybe flamethrowers would work since it shied from Rose's flames, but...

This is the sort of situation where Alice's brains are our best bet.

However, Alice shakes her head as everyone naturally turns to look at her.

"I don't have enough intel on that mole. Since we don't know what'll work, save your Evil Points. For now, I'll try setting traps with materials from this planet, but don't expect too much from them. Things like rockets, anti-materiel-rifle rounds, grenades, and sonic depth charges elicit a reaction if they connect, but they all lack that final punch. Still, there's something off about that mole's defenses. I won't accept the existence of something as far-fetched as defensive magic, but we do need to explore every avenue we can."

As Alice willfully refutes the possibility of the supernatural, the agents start to grumble.

"So you're saying you've got nothing. Given how you're always ordering us around, you need to be better about putting that brain to work when we need it."

Surprisingly, Alice nods to that.

"All right… Well, I wasn't going to suggest this at first, but we could always arm each of you with an R-Buzzsaw and have you charge in. Those would likely do some damage. I mean, losing a few Combat Agents doesn't hurt Kisaragi in the slightest, so how about we try that?"

"Don't give her any ideas! She's got command authority during war, remember? If she says to do it, we'll actually have to!"

"So you're saying we're expendable, you merciless rust bucket?!"

"That's beyond cruel! Combat Agents are people, too! Our lives are precious!"

"I'm sorry for teasing you! So please—anything but that!"

By the time the meeting is finally over, it seems the sun has set. It's getting to be nighttime…

In the deserted cafeteria, Snow, who's been dragged into all this, is picking on Viper.

"Why do I have to help defeat the Sand King?! Princess Tillis did mention something about our kingdom's reputation suffering if Kisaragi eliminated it on their own, but…"

"I'm sorry! You have my sincerest apologies! I'm so very sorry!"

Despite the fact that she can't hold her liquor, Snow has Viper pouring her drinks. One sip of sake later…

"Mmm, that's goo— I mean, this is rancid! A drink poured by a Demon Lord is unpalatable!"

"I'm sorry, I'm sorry! Sh-should I bring you some beer instead…?"

Viper doesn't break under Snow's bullying and instead moves to fetch some beer, but…

"Oh, no, this is fine. No need to put yourself out! Tch, because you inherited the throne, my Demon Lord intel was useless, and I missed my chance for glory! How are you going to take responsibility?!"

"I'm sorry for inheriting the throne without your permission! Oh… Your cup is empty; should I refrain from refilling it…?"

Snow turns to Viper, who's been taking care of her despite the harassment.

"Of course you should refill the empty cup! But right now, it's time for you to drink!"

"V-very well, I'll have some…"

Snow's turned into an aggressive drunk, switching between saying sake poured by a Demon Lord is undrinkable and then demanding a refill, but…

"I've had lots of dear subordinates die in battle against the Demon Lord's Army, but if you drink all that up, I, Snow the Magnanimous, will forgive you! Show your appreciation!"

"Th-thank you very much! I will have this drink as the representative of all demons…!"

She's a drunk, but she's also a former knight captain who commanded a lot of troops. I suppose she's still working through some bitter feelings toward the demons.

Viper herself doesn't seem to mind, so I guess I'll leave them be.

"Boff, you're not gonna help Miff Fiper?" asks Rose with a full mouth as I watch Snow and Viper.

"Vi has this tendency to occasionally seek atonement for the past, so maybe getting hazed a little helps her. If you see another agent bullying Vi, though, you can go ahead and chew on them."

"Understood. If Ms. Viper gets sexually harassed by someone, I'll make sure to chomp on them."

I nod to Rose's reassuring words and sip my beer.

Eventually, the cafeteria empties out, and as I look around and get ready to leave…

*   *   *

...the hideout quakes.

"The mole's back. Everyone, grab an R-Buzzsaw and assemble in the courtyard outside the hideout. If anyone's still sleeping, slap them awake!"

Alice's broadcast rings through the base, and at the same time, the sounds of footfalls echo through the halls.

Something about the specific order to grab an R-Buzzsaw bugs me, but I take mine, which is propped up against the table.

"Time to go mole hunting! Let's show them the power of the former Grace Kingdom Skirmish Squad!"

"Boss, Snow blacked out from drinking too much! Also, Grimm's still resurrecting!"

Why are my squad members so useless when I need them?!

With no other choice, I head out with only Rose in tow, but to my surprise, Viper tags along.

"What are you doing, Vi? It's dangerous. You should stay in the hideout."

"No, as the former Demon Lord, it's my responsibility to see the demons to safety. I'm still their leader. I think I can be of use to you, Mr. Six..."

...She can't shake my worry, though. This girl's seriously self-sacrificing. She probably wouldn't hesitate to throw her life away if it meant saving someone else...

"...You're late, Six. You're the last one here. I'm not surprised that Grimm is absent, but where the hell is Snow?"

Arriving on the scene, I see the agents have surrounded the mole and are holding out long sticks.

"Snow blacked out, so I left her behind. What are they doing?"

The long sticks the agents are wielding are shaped like spoons, and there's something piled on the ends of them.

"We're drawing its attention with food while we evacuate the demons. It wasn't hard to guess what kind of food a mole would like. I whipped up a blend that it should find particularly appetizing."

Alice starts to write something while she speaks.

I'm curious, so I sneak a peek and see she's writing about Snow...

Looks like it's a report to Tillis.

I guess she plans to use Snow's screwup as a way to get concessions from Tillis during the negotiations.

"If we have bait that moles like, it should be easy enough to prepare a trap. Should we try laying land mines or something?"

"That'll be a last resort. After all, you agents never remember where you bury your mines. I can say with absolute certainty one of you will end up stepping on one by mistake."

True, all agents except me are pretty stupid.

We're talking about a group of guys who might very well be dumber than a mole. There's a good chance they really would step on their own land mines.

The Sand King, lit by a spotlight, shows interest in the bait. Its nose is twitching this way and that.

"I've mixed a powerful sedative into the bait. Once it falls asleep, we'll have the upper hand. Finishing it off after that shouldn't be too bad."

Alice says this without much conviction, but she's forgetting something important.

"This is a boss monster. It's impervious to status effects."

That's something any RPG gamer would know.

If we could solve the problem with sedatives, that'd be a little too easy.

Alice freezes for a moment, but then says with exasperation:

"...Really? A 'boss monster'? I know you think of everything as a video game, but this is reality. It's time to get a grip."

"No, you're the one who needs to get a grip, Alice. Even if we're talking about elite demons or whatever, a tranquilizer gun would be the ultimate weapon, but I've never tried using a weapon like that, have I?"

"......I guess you can use your head a little when it comes to battle. I figured the reason you didn't use sleeping gas or tranquilizers was because we hadn't confirmed if Earth-derived chemicals would work on this planet's creatures."

Still, depending on the game, certain status effects *can* work on boss monsters.

Before charging in with my R-Buzzsaw, I can just wait until the Sand King eats the bait. At least then, we'll know if it'll even work or not.

"...Huh. It sniffed at the bait, but it doesn't look like it's going for it. See? It's a boss immunity! This is probably why status effects don't work in video games!"

"Don't be ridiculous. I picked chemicals with no flavor or scent... Wait a sec. I included worms and bugs into the mix because it's a mole, but..."

The Sand King turns up its nose at the offered bait, approaches a nearby Combat Agent, and...

Chomp.

"Gyaaaaaaah! My anti-materiel rifle! ...Th-this thing's not looking at the bait. It's looking at me..."

The Combat Agent shoved his anti-materiel rifle forward when he dodged the Sand King's attack, resulting in the mole munching on that instead.

The Sand King chews for a moment before spitting something onto the ground.

The agents all fall silent at the sight of the small lump of steel that used to be a gun.

"...Well, given its size, I guess there's no reason for it to fixate on small insects. If it can eat bugs, then it can eat other living creatures. Given that it didn't hesitate to snap at the agent, it must already have a taste for people," says Alice.

"Why are you so damn calm?! That thing might look cute, but it's super dangerous!"

I draw my R-Buzzsaw while admonishing Alice's trademark apathy.

"Let's go. I'll draw its attention, so give it a good slashing! Everyone, ready your R-Buzzsaws!"

Taking the lead as this planet's manager, I dash off toward the Sand King.

...Chaaaarge!

2

"*Squeesqueesqueek!*"

"*Hisssss!*"

The giant Sand King makes oddly cute mewling noises, while Rose bares her fangs to intimidate it.

Having had part of my power armor torn open by the Sand King, I decide I've done enough as a decoy. I'm hanging out next to Alice.

"Sorry, Alice. Rose wouldn't have to face off alone against it if I could've bought a few more minutes..."

"There's nothing to do about that. You did well enough."

I use my downtime to observe the battle.

Thanks to my perfect performance as a decoy, the Sand King's covered in injuries. It's squeaking as Rose keeps it restrained.

Even though bullets and harpoons didn't work, the attacks with R-Buzzsaws definitely did damage.

Does that mean the only plan we've got is a suicide charge of Combat Agents with R-Buzzsaws?

...Just then, Rose strikes a weird pose and sucks in a deep breath.

"Drown in my hellfire! Sleep for eternity! Crimson Breaaaath!"

"Squee! Squeesqueee!"

Although the Sand King's getting bathed in flame, it doesn't seem to be taking any damage. I guess it does have some fire resistance after all.

Turning its back to Rose, it flicks up dirt with its claw.

"Bwah! Ack! I got dirt in my mouth...!"

As Rose is blanketed by dirt, letting out a cry as she defends her face...

"Squee!"

"Guuuh!"

...she gets sent flying by one of the Sand King's flailing limbs.

Catching Rose in midair, I roll to kill our momentum.

Fortunately, it didn't pierce her with a claw, and I don't see any wounds on her.

"I'm sorry, but my body hurts too much to move. This is frustrating..."

"Rest here a bit. Like me, you did well. Good job... As for the rest of you, try harder! Fight at least as hard as Rose and I did!"

"Yes, yes, Six. You fought hard."

I guess the Sand King really does have sharp senses, because it keeps attacking in the direction it hears the slightest noise coming from, so until the demons finish evacuating, we've been yelling back and forth to draw its attention.

The Combat Agents scurrying around the Sand King start yelling at us.

"Hey, Alice, stop babying Six! He didn't even last ten seconds as a decoy. All he did was get hit and then run away!"

"Oh, shut up! Then you be the decoy! I'm special to Alice. My efforts and results are things only Alice understands. Ain't that right, partner?"

"It's because you do what I say when I give you a little encouragement. There, there. Well done. I have something else I need you to take care of."

Alice then lightly pats my head.

For some reason, I have a bad feeling about this.

Just as I'm contemplating making my escape before anything happens...

"We've finished evacuating the demons! I apologize for the delay! I'll be lending my assistance now!"

In a situation where the Combat Agents are staying back because of claws that can easily tear through power armor, Viper dashes over, heaving labored breaths.

Feeling their masculinity threatened by the incredibly powerful women before them, my colleagues close the distance with the Sand King.

With the evacuation of the demons complete, Alice issues an order to an agent with good sniping skills.

"Try shooting a cutting round into the Sand King."

The agent unslings his rifle and, as instructed, loads a cutting round designed for slashing ropes from long distance.

He fires at the Sand King, but a moment later, the shot gets deflected off the seemingly impenetrable hide without leaving a scratch, then rebounds back to the agent who fired it, grazing his head.

"So R-Buzzsaws work, but it doesn't look like it's particularly vulnerable to cutting attacks..."

"Hey, Alice, that almost took my head off! Show a little more concern for our lives, please!"

As Mr. Expendable whines, Alice looks up.

"I think I'm on to something. Six, go punch the Sand King."

The android, whom I previously thought of as a genius, is turning out to be just as useless as her creator.

"As a surgically enhanced human, my punch is strong, sure, but it won't do anything against an enemy *that* big. Besides, getting close to a giant, pissed-off mole is just asking for death."

I shake my head and shrug my shoulders, but Alice just makes a shooing gesture at me.

"Forget all that and get to it already. If you keep refusing, I'll use my command authority."

"You tyrant! After I get a hit in, I'm booking it!"

I look to the Sand King after filing my last complaint with Alice.

There's nothing more dangerous than a wounded wild animal.

The Sand King sniffs around before lashing out with its claws the moment it hears movement.

Eventually, it looks directly at me, and we lock eyes.

As I freeze in place, Alice yells over at me.

"You moron! There's no point crawling toward an opponent who doesn't rely on eyesight. Hurry and stand up!"

Distracted by Alice's voice, the Sand King whiffs its claw attack over the top of my head.

"Whoa, that was close! Why can't you tell me these things ahead of time?!"

As I flee back toward Alice, she gives me a look of utter disappointment.

"It's my fault for not considering your complete lack of intelligence... Do we have anyone with the guts to go land a punch on the Sand King?!"

I don't think there's anyone here with a weird enough fetish that they'd happily run toward an enemy that deadly...

"I'll go."

After saying this in a low voice, Viper runs in.

"Vi, what are you doing?! You guys, cover her! We'll draw the Sand King's attention!"

As Viper quickly closes in on her target, we decide to distract it instead of trying to stop her.

"Hey! Hey, over here, you stupid mole! Look at meeee!"

"I know it won't work, but take this! Don't underestimate an enhanced agent's fastball!"

"Keep taunting it! I know it won't understand our words, but taunt it anyway! You damned mole! Your beady eyes are so adorable! Stop twitching that nose!"

Some agents jeer, and others start throwing rocks.

Seemingly annoyed by all the noise we're making, the Sand King, now with a decent grasp of where everyone is, turns its nose toward our group...

"Demon Lord Punch!" yells Viper as she delivers a mighty kick to the Sand King.

"...Did that do it?"

"Damn, the Demon Lord Punch is awesome! Even if it's not a punch!"

"Wow, so that's the power of a Demon Lord! That totally wasn't a punch, though! It was a flying kick!"

As the agents get worked up, the Sand King snaps out of its daze.

It definitely looks like it's in pain where Viper kicked it, and as it gets up, it seems to be protecting its flank.

I guess a single "Demon Lord Punch" wasn't enough to take it down.

But Alice knew that'd be the case, so what's she after?

"You guys, engage it in melee combat! The Sand King's using some mysterious energy to nullify ranged attacks. Strike it with something other than projectile weapons!" shouts Alice confidently.

"Mysterious energy"? It's weird for her, of all people, to say something like that.

"What's up, Alice? Are you describing things in video-game

terms now, too? We'll have to get you in character, then. First, you need to call me something like *master* or *owner*. After that, just throw in some robot noises every now and then, and you'll be perfect."

"...What are you talking about? This is a boss immunity. You mentioned boss monsters are sometimes immune to things like status effects, right? The Sand King is using something that greatly nullifies ranged attacks, though I'm not sure what."

Come to think of it, Rose's fire breath only had an effect at close range.

That means her order to go punch the Sand King was to confirm that hypothesis.

"I see. So it has the magical barrier that someone mentioned at the meeting."

"There's no such thing as magical barriers. It's a mysterious energy. Remember when Tiger Man mentioned punching it seemed to work? Viper's Demon Lord Punch and the slashes from the R-Buzzsaws are also melee attacks. Meaning...harpoons might work if they're not thrown but stabbed into its flesh at close range."

Alice stubbornly denies the existence of magic, but listening to our exchange, Viper picks up a discarded harpoon.

"Vi?! You've done enough! Vi, come back, Vi!"

As Viper charges in again, the Sand King looks frightened.

The Demon Lord Punch must have hurt a lot, because it won't take its attention off Viper even as loud noises echo all around it.

The Sand King rears up and brings down its front legs just as Viper jumps in and drives the harpoon into its belly.

The Sand King screeches in agony, but as it moves to strike Viper, its claws just barely miss her hair.

"Everyone, request harpoons! As you can see, they'll work if you get close!"

At Alice's words, the mood of the agents changes.

Now that its weakness has been confirmed, it's our time to shine.

Just as everyone's morale rises—

"Skreeeeeeeeee!"

—the Sand King lets out a sharp, high-pitched squeal and dives into the hole from which it emerged.

3

"What were you thinking, Vi? Can you stop doing that sort of thing?"

"I'm sorry, I'm sorry! My apologies! It's my fault that we let the Sand King get away…!"

We finally finish patching everyone up after the Sand King's escape.

I'm lecturing Viper in the hideout's conference room.

"That's not important right now! Look, Vi, do you have any idea how rare you are? You're a ten out of ten, you have common sense, and you have no weird quirks to speak of! Your life is way more valuable than a bunch of Combat Agents whose numbers could honestly use a little thinning. Please don't go eagerly running to your death!"

"U-umm…"

Viper looks troubled by my overly serious lecture.

"Hey, do you think Six said all that knowing he's a Combat Agent, too?"

"Well, it's a given that Ms. Viper's life is more valuable than Six's, but I still can't go along with what he said…"

The expendables are grousing as they eavesdrop on my lecture, but suddenly, Alice drops some documents onto the desk.

"I know you're exhausted since we just drove the Sand King off, but there's no guarantee it won't be back tonight. It's best to get this sort of thing out of the way early. I'm going to summarize the plan for you goons."

Now that we've figured out the Sand King's special ability, we have plenty of ways to deal with it.

Given that it's been doing as it pleases up until now, it's our turn to do some damage.

"As it says in the documents in front of you, the cost of training a single Combat Agent is this. Now, the advantages that'll come from defeating the Sand King, when converted into money, is about that."

Alice speaks breezily, but I feel nothing but dread about where this is going.

I mean, why would she explain how much we cost?

"The plan is super simple. Everyone grabs a harpoon, charges, and after affixing the ropes, we cut off its escape and kill it. Calculating from its ability to swat away construction equipment, we'll need to spear it with about fifty harpoons to hold it down. The expected number of casualties among the agents is…around three. The upsides more than outweigh the downsides, so there's nothing to fear. Dismissed!"

"'Dismissed' my ass! Come up with a plan where we don't end up dying!"

"You're supposed to be a high-spec genius, right?! Please, Alice, I beg you—come up with something where there's no losses!"

"Don't go putting prices on our lives in the first place! And for crying out loud, the number on this document is way too low!"

As the expendables whine, I speak up for Alice.

"Pipe down, you grunts! You're Combat Agents! Your value exists in your ability to risk your lives on the front lines. If you're so afraid of dying, then go ahead and quit, you cowards!"

"Oh? Big words from the guy who was the first to flee today!"

"You seem to be under the impression that you're special, Six. You're still a Combat Agent, you know! You're gonna have to take up a harpoon and try to stab the Sand King, too!"

They really do get angry too easily. But this isn't the time to mince words.

"I'm this base's branch manager, remember? We are not the same! There's no way in hell I'm gonna participate in a plan that dangerous, and even if I wanted to, I'm sure Alice would stop me. Understand the difference in our ranks, peons!"

As I put the underlings in their place, they begin quaking in red-faced rage.

Oh, they're looking mighty aggressive today.

"All right, you guys want a fight? Then come on. You're all exhausted from taking on the mole, while I just sat there and watched for the most part. You know who'd have the advantage, right…?"

Before I can finish, Alice interjects:

"Six, you'll be leading them from the front."

……

"I'm sorry, what was that?"

"You heard me. You're going to be the first one in. You're still using the old-style power armor, meaning you're the toughest one here, and you've got the highest chance of survival. While Combat Agents are a dime a dozen, if we can keep the losses to a minimum, that'd be preferable."

Wai—!

"Hold on, my power armor's nothing to write home about! You saw what happened! The Sand King tore through it like paper! Besides, I need to send my power armor out for repairs first…"

"Leave the repairs to me. Power armor is something Lady Lilith created, so I can fix a suit in a single night, even with the facilities we have here."

Why is she so useful now of all times?!

"C'mon, partner, come up with a safer plan, please! I know you can do it if you put your mind to it. Surely, there's something that'll work better!"

"Stop whining, Six! Get it together!"

"Yeah, show us what it means to be a branch manager, sir!"

While thinking about how best to punish my comrades' taunts, I hear a demure voice coming from behind me.

"Um... In that case, I can charge in first..."

The speaker is none other than Viper.

"Oh, don't be ridiculous, Vi! I told you to stop leaping into harm's way!"

"Y-yes, but...defeating the Sand King is the long-held desire of all demons. If the demons show they're also willing to put their lives on the line to defeat the Sand King, that would likely help the kingdom of Grace feel a bit better about letting us settle here..."

As ever, her logic is sound.

Still, is there really a need for Viper, the former Demon Lord, to enter the fray?

From the moment we first met, I've been getting a certain vibe from her...

"...Well, fine. If Viper's participating, I can't allow her to get hurt, no matter how small the chance of that happening actually is. Looks like I'll have to bring out my precious tiger cub."

Alice's words throw me right off my train of thought.

"...What was that about Tiger Man?"

"I didn't say anything about Tiger Man. He wandered off without telling us. Usually, going AWOL like that makes one subject to heavy punishment."

Yes, we still haven't been able to find Tiger Man ever since the first Sand King attack.

With that said, it's not an unusual thing for Tiger Man to wander off when he feels like it.

"Tiger Man has feline DNA. That wanderlust is part of his nature. He can't help it."

"If we allowed mutants to indulge in their bestial natures, you would've been eaten by Spider Woman and Mantis Woman a long time ago."

She means that sexually…right?

Rose is already one hyperliteral carnivore too many.

…Just then.

The meeting-room door opens, and a person carrying something on his back walks in.

"Hey, guys! Sorrrry to keep you waiting."

With auspicious timing, the one strolling through the door is none other than Tiger Man.

I don't know where he's been, but he looks pretty beat-up.

"Hey, Tiger Man's back! And get a load of him! I bet he was off training to get strong enough to beat the Sand King!"

"I see. We can throw Tiger Man at the Sand King, then. That just might work."

As the agents all buzz around him, Tiger Man tilts his head.

"What are you talking about? I had a pretty specific goal in mind when I left… Ms. Viper."

"Y-yes? Wh-what is it?"

As Tiger Man addresses her with an expression so serious that he forgets his usual purring, Viper, who has been serving tea to everyone, looks up in surprise.

"I have a purresent for you!"

With that, he hands Viper an item that he pulled from his backpack.

"…Is this a sorcerer stone? I've never seen one this big. It must have been absorbing magical energy for a long, long time. I can feel an immense power radiating from it…! But why would you give something like this to me…?"

As she raises the question, Tiger Man gives his straitlaced reply.

"This is a sorcerer stone I won from a mighty dragon. Ms. Viper, with this powerful artifact…could you possibly return me to my childhood?"

"I'm sorry. I can't."

The immediacy of her reply drives Tiger Man to a corner, where he curls up into a ball.

"What're we gonna do, Alice? Your tiger cub's depressed!"

"Dammit! Game over, man! Game over!"

"I'm sorry, I'm sorry, it's all my fault, I'm so sorry!"

The conference room descends into chaos, and Alice attempts to ease our panic.

"Calm down, you morons. I already told you that when I mentioned my 'tiger cub,' I wasn't talking about Tiger Man. Come with me, and you'll see what I'm talking about."

Alice brings us to the mystery facility that was recently built near the hideout.

No one knows what it is, and since it often sounds like there's someone crying inside, we Combat Agents steer clear of the place. If there were ghosts about, there wouldn't be a damn thing any of us could do.

"Alice, leave this place alone. There have been reports of a sobbing woman's voice coming from here every night. One rumor tells of a woman, driven to depression over her failure in love, killing herself and haunting this place..."

"Every time I think you all can't possibly get any stupider... The construction on our base was only recently completed. How the hell would those rumors even make sense?"

Alice rolls her eyes at us and opens the door to the mystery facility.

...As it opens, we hear a woman crying.

With the rumors partway confirmed, we struggle to choke down our fear as we peer inside.

Heine of the Flames, former pillar of the Demon Lord's Elite Four, sobs as she produces fire from her hand.

*   *   *

"This is the power plant for Hideout City. You noticed Mr. Destroyer resting next to it, yeah? Since we got acquired Heine in our recent deal, I built a thermal power plant to take full advantage of her abilities."

What an awful facility. Leave it to an android to be completely devoid of pity or mercy.

Having noticed our presence, Heine continues making flames but turns to face us as she weeps.

"I don't want to make fire anymore! Help me, Six, please! I'm tired of spending all my time here boiling water!"

Heine is so broken that she's rejecting her very identity as a fire demon.

"Oh, so this is where you were. Congrats! You're being evaluated for your abilities, and not your sex appeal!"

"Even a lewd job is preferable to doing this forever! ...S-sorry, that was a lie. I lied, so stop looking at me like that..."

Heine shies away from the hungry, predatory gazes of my colleagues.

Oh, right, our electricity restrictions ended when Heine started working here.

Thinking about it that way, maybe relieving her of this job wouldn't be such a great thing...

But as Heine complains, Alice offers a comment.

"Shut up and keep generating. Once you've completely recharged Mr. Destroyer, I'll let you take one out of every ten days off. And I'll cut you down to fifteen work hours a day."

Those are some harsh working conditions, but for some reason, Heine's expression brightens.

"R-really?! You're not lying, right? I'm choosing to believe you!"

Heine's delight at those heinous conditions is really bumming me out.

…Wait, come to think of it, given that we risk our lives on a constant basis, don't get any days off on long-term missions, and often have to scrounge for our own survival, a Combat Agent has pretty crappy working conditions, too…

"So how much longer will I have to make fire before Mr. Destroyer is recharged?"

"At this rate, it shouldn't take much longer than a week."

And just like that, Heine crumples, her sliver of happiness lost to the void.

However, an unexpected beacon of hope presents itself.

"Um… Why don't we have Heine use this…?"

Viper then hesitantly produces the sorcerer stone that she received from Tiger Man. Upon seeing it, Heine's eyes go wide with shock.

"Wh-what a powerful sorcerer stone…! Lady Viper, where did you find such a thing…?" asks Heine as she takes the stone in her hands.

"Tiger Man said he got it from a dragon…"

"A dra—?! S-surely, you jest… Dragons are immensely powerful creatures that may even be mightier than the Sand or Forest Kings. How could he have possibly…?"

Oh, right, I did kind of gloss over this earlier, but yeah—dragons are more or less the rulers of all monsters…

…and any Kisaragi operative would know exactly how a mutant like Tiger Man managed to beat one.

Mutants are able to become giant versions of themselves if they're pushed to the brink of death.

It's a trump card that heavily depletes their own vitality, and it's the reason why the Heroes started building stuff like giant robots.

I guess Tiger Man *really* wanted to be a kid again.

I can't really sympathize in the slightest, but I do admire his dedication.

"Lady Viper, thank you very much. With this, I can create some enormous flames… And, Six, I'll show you the real power of a former pillar of the Demon Lord's Elite Four!"

Heine puts on a radiant smile as she burns bright with confidence.

4

The day after Heine shows her commitment.

"Too hot!"

Inside the newly boosted power plant, Heine, slick with sweat, makes note of the obvious.

The flames she was able to produce by combining her full focus with the dragon's sorcerer stone were impressive.

How impressive, you ask? So impressive that she was able to raise the temperature of Hideout City by several degrees.

And even more impressive is…

"…What do you mean, 'too hot'? Aren't you the pillar of the Elite Four who's dedicated to fire?"

…Heine. Her glistening, sun-kissed curves are too alluring for words.

In video games, her sort of character usually gets a lot more energetic in extreme heat.

"What are you talking about? Russell would drown if you sank him in a pond. I mean, sure, I have a bit more fire resistance than your average demon, but…there's a reason I dress like this, you know."

Heine then motions to herself rather suggestively.

"You dress provocatively so that your enemies lower their guards, right? Our female mutants do the same thing, more or less."

"No, you idiot! I wear less because fire is *hot*! If I wore layers, and they caught on fire, that'd be a huge problem!"

Oh. And here I thought she was supposed to be "the sexy one" among the Elite Four. I guess her outfit had a more pragmatic purpose.

…For some reason, Snow then turns her gaze away, as though faintly uncomfortable.

"What's the reasoning behind *your* outfit, Snow?"

"…Because the orcs and goblins that make up the bulk of the Demon Lord's Army prefer to take women as prisoners rather than kill them. If you increase the amount of skin that's showing, they do their best to avoid damaging their prey, and it raises the chances of survival. The reason our kingdom's female soldiers don't wear helmets is to let the enemy know they're women."

All right, now *that* sounds a lot more like what Kisaragi's female mutants do.

"H-hey! Stop talking like orcs and goblins are sexual deviants! They're actually pretty nice guys on the whole. Even then, I can't believe you're using the fact that you're a woman as a weapon. How shady…"

"There's nothing shady in war! What's wrong with using everything at our disposal when our lives are on the line?! Besides, you yourself use your gender as a weapon as well!"

Not wanting to enter the sweltering power plant, Snow points at Heine from the safety of the doorway.

"I-I'm using my womanhood as a weapon?! As if! Where's your proof?!"

"The fact that you're still alive is all the proof I need! If you were a man, Six wouldn't have let you escape all those times we fought! He would've finished you off a long time ago!"

At those words, Heine glares at me.

"Hey, Six, answer me. If I were—"

"If you were a guy, I obviously would've never hesitated to kill you. Kisaragi already has too many dudes as it is. I've even openly said I'd be totally fine if we culled some of our other agents."

I answer before she finishes her question, and Heine looks thoroughly taken aback.

"...I see. I guess I should be more appreciative that I'm a woman... *Sigh*. Still, it really is hot in here. My goodness..."

Heine slumps her shoulders and returns to work.

"So why are you here anyway? There's no need to keep an eye on me. The promise of *slightly* better treatment is motivation enough. Plus, once I finish charging this thing, we'll be able to take down the Sand King, right? If we can really kill that bastard, I'm going to pour all my efforts into getting us the opportunity."

Heine then holds out her hands to produce more fire.

"I don't have anything else to do, so I figured I'd come appreciate your glistening ass."

"Get outta here! You're a bother, so leave! And stop looking at my ass!"

Heine peppers me with insults, but she's currently a slave. There's no need for me to do as she asks.

As I plop down on the ground and continue ogling her, Heine lets out an exasperated sigh.

"...This imbecile aside, why are *you* here?"

Snow smirks at Heine's words.

"I heard you were being worked to the bone, so I thought I'd come see. As a knight of the kingdom of Grace, I have a duty to defend the country. Since I can't trust demons, I'm not going to relax my vigilance in watching you."

"You speak of duty, but weren't you blackout drunk yesterday when the Sand King attacked?"

Sweat beads on Snow's brow at my remark, and she fans herself in an exaggerated manner to try to distract from it.

"Wow, it sure is hot in here... A frozen dessert would hit the spot, I bet. I got one from the cafeteria short while ago, but I heard they taste better in a hot room like this."

…Ohhh, now I get why she's here.

"A frozen dessert…? H-hey, don't eat that in here. Or at least, do it where I can't see you!"

"I can eat what I want, when I want, where I want! Oh, do you want some?"

Snow scoops a spoonful of ice cream, then pops it in her mouth in front of Heine's eyes.

Then, she takes out a second spoon that she went to the trouble of obtaining, scoops up some more ice cream, and slowly moves the spoon toward Heine's mouth.

"Here, open wide."

Snow smiles and offers the ice cream with a gentle tone.

"Huh?! O-oh, b-but, um… Okay then, aaahhh…"

The treat melts before it even touches Heine's lips.

"Whoa! That's impressive, Heine of the Flames! Your flames are so powerful that the ice cream melted!"

"…I'll eat it myself, so hand that over."

"I was only going to give you one bite. And that bite already melted. Ha-ha-ha-ha-ha-ha! That expression! That's the real treat! Entertain me more!"

As Heine trembles with rage, Snow clutches her sides and howls with laughter.

I mean, sure, they have a history that includes melting one of Snow's swords, but still, what a sadist.

…Not that I'm one to talk, but man, Snow's totally rotten to the core. She might be beyond saving.

"What the hell, you two?! Right now, I'm working hard so that you can defeat the Sand King! I'm telling Alice that you're getting in my way!"

Dammit, she's only been here a few days, and she already knows the power dynamics of this place.

Snow and I exchange glances and nod…

"We'll let you go today. Make sure you show your ass off more tomorrow!"

"I need you to work as hard as my poor, melted blade. Prepare for more teasing tomorrow!"

Making remarks that sound vaguely like thuggish threats, we exit the power plant.

?? month/?? day

Heine snitched, and Alice cut off my allowance.

I'm back at the power plant to give Heine a piece of my mind, but...

"Well, well, you really did it this time, Heine. Thanks to you, Alice cut me off."

"Tch, yeah. Alice told me to either pay everything I owe her immediately or to kneel and prostrate myself before her, so I wound up bowing and worshipping her when I didn't want to."

"Y-you receive an allowance from a child...? Also, there's something weird about owing a kid so much money that you have no choice but to worship them..."

Heine's totally repulsed, but this is all her fault to begin with.

"You make it sound as if you had nothing to do with it, but we're here to take our revenge."

"Yeah, I hope you're ready. Heh-heh. Demons are the enemy! All right, Six, bring it out!"

At Snow's command, I produce the space heater I grabbed from the hideout.

Heine tilts her head quizzically as she continues producing flames.

"Do you know what this is, Heine? This is state-of-the-art heating equipment from my planet!"

"It's hot in here right now, but we're about to make it even hotter! Heh-heh-heh. But hey, you're an elite fire demon, right? It's not like you're gonna beg us to stop, riiiiight?"

As we squat in front of the space heater and flash smug grins at Heine, she wears a faintly perplexed expression.

"Have you learned nothing from yesterday? If you interrupt me, Alice is going to get mad at you again. Or have you come up with some sort of good excuse this time?"

"Heh-heh, the mistake is assuming we're here to interrupt your work. All we're doing is enjoying the warmth of this facility. Where we warm ourselves up has nothing to do with you, no?"

"Exactly. This isn't hazing; we're just trying to stay warm. Ha-ha-ha! Don't underestimate human intellect! Just sit there and suffer, Heine of the Flames!"

Heine stands there frozen in shock, likely blown away by the brilliance of our plan.

Ten minutes later.

"...Hey, are you two okay? Your faces are all red, and you're sweating like crazy. I think you're getting dehydrated."

Heine's sweating a little bit, but Snow and I are about to pass out.

"...Why do you seem so unfazed?"

"I'm hot, too. But I already told you I have some natural fire resistance... Um, are you sure she's okay?"

Hearing that, I look over at Snow and notice she's got a thousand-yard stare going on, and her face is red as a chili pepper.

I have power armor that helps regulate my body temperature for environments with extreme weather, but I'm pretty sure Snow's nearing the danger zone.

Snow snaps out of her stupor when she hears us talking about her, but she must've realized the dangerous game she was playing because she stands up in a hurry.

"Y-you're off the hook for today! ...Let's go, Six! If we stay in here any longer, we'll die!"

"Dammit! I'll get you next time!"

I fire a verbal parting shot straight from the Kisaragi manual, scoop up Snow, who's swaying from side to side, grab the heater, and leave.

The moment we step through the door, I hear Heine mutter to herself.

"...I lost to *these guys*...?"

?? month/?? day

"I brought something nice for you. Heine, how are you faring? Is the work tolerable?"

Viper comes in to cheer up Heine, bearing ice cream.

"Lady Viper, I'm all right for now! I've started to get used to the heat, and I've even gotten permission to burn a couple of insects the next time they interrupt my work."

Heine points in my direction when she mentions the "insects." Seeming satisfied with herself, she puts on a cheery smile and takes a bite of the ice cream.

"These people may be immeasurably cruel and heartless, but their food sure is tasty, isn't it, Lady Viper?"

"Yes, their food is good. But I think they're nice people, Heine."

As Viper exhibits her total lack of perception, I debate whether or not I should voice my agreement.

Heine may have undying loyalty to Viper, but this is one thing she can't bend on.

"So what are you doing here, Mr. Six?"

"I'm watching Heine... That's an excuse, though. I just figured if I was here, the other agents wouldn't harass her. They're starving for women, so there's no telling what they'd do."

"You're the most dangerous one from where I'm standing... Wait, where are you looking...?"

Even against Heine's rude remark, I don't avert my gaze.

"Your ass, of course. I mean, you can't put the goods on display and then complain when I check out the merchandise. You're practically wearing a swimsuit. Now that you're a Kisaragi slave, that ass is ours for the ogling."

"Hey, no, stop staring. My butt is my own... Lady Viper, will you still claim they're all good people after hearing that? This man's worthless. I'd stay far away from him if I were you."

Viper simply chuckles at our back-and-forth.

"You two seem to be getting along rather famously to me."

"Lady Viper, you can't be serious. This man is my enemy."

"All right, come at me. Even though you're our lowest-ranking member, it looks like you still don't know your place," I say to Heine.

Heine's right, though. Viper's *really* bad at reading people.

When I was with Rose, Viper mentioned something about us acting like siblings. Maybe she's just been too sheltered to know any better.

"...Really? You think that you, a mere human, can beat me now that I have a dragon's sorcerer stone?"

"Oops, you said 'mere human.' That's one of the lines forbidden by the Kisaragi manual. You just doomed yourself to lose."

......

"I don't quite know you're talking about, but I know you're making fun of me. Well if you're going that far, step right up. I'll vaporize you using my dragon's sorcerer stone!"

"Oh yeah?! I've got the former Demon Lord Vi on my side! I won't lose to a former Elite Four member like you!"

"Whaaat?!"

Viper lets out a cry of surprise as she's suddenly added into the fight like it's the most natural thing in the world.

"Wh-why would Lady Viper get involved?! This is a one-on-one duel between you and me!"

I affectionately wrap my arm around Viper's shoulder.

"Vi, Vi, your former subordinate keeps picking a fight with me. Can you give her a stern talking-to? Right now, I can only sleep at night. I'm too afraid of her randomly attacking me to sleep any other time."

"Ummm... Heine, please don't pick on Mr. Six..."

"Lady Viper, please don't be fooled by his random words! *He's* the one who comes to pick on *me*! And damn you, Six, don't casually touch Lady Viper like that! If you keep interrupting my work, I'll tell Alice!" Heine protests, cheeks flushed. Having her telling Alice would be a problem.

"All right, fine. You're off the hook for now. Vi, I'm bored. Will you play with me? The usual, of course. Just the two of us."

"Yes, gladly!"

As I try to leave with the now-beaming Viper, Heine calls after us.

"L-Lady Viper? Um, what does he mean when he says 'play' and 'the usual' with 'just the two of us'?"

With my arm around Viper's shoulder, I turn to Heine, who looks nervous all of a sudden.

"It's not a big deal. We do all sorts of things together, and Viper shows me the ropes. It'll be nice to get this craving outta my system, so let's get a move on."

"Yes, let's. I wasn't very confident in my ability at first, but I've really been enjoying myself lately."

"...?!"

?? month/?? day

One of the dime-a-dozen agents lets out a yelp.

"Oh my god! Ms. Heine is so damn sexy!"

The power plant—my little slice of heaven—is now filled with Combat Agents slacking off.

"Damn... A busty, dark-skinned demon beauty getting all sweaty..."

"I'm so glad I came to this planet... I don't think I want to go back to Earth anymore."

Hearing the untoward observations, Heine pumps out flames as though taking her frustration out on the boiler.

Near her, cackling with great satisfaction is—

"Ha-ha-ha-ha-ha! Look at all this money, Six! You have to admit this is a genius business plan!"

Snow cradles the box of money she made selling tickets to the Heine show.

I have to admit, it was a pretty good scheme.

Heine, begrudgingly staying on task, lets out a whisper.

"...Just so we're clear, if you're going to use my ass to make money, you better give me a cut."

It looks like she's given up on trying to prevent people from looking, and now she's angling for a piece of the pie for herself.

As expected from a former pillar of the Elite Four. She's tougher than I've been giving her credit for.

During the exchange between Snow and Heine, the expendables politely sit in a row and to watch attentively.

"I think I'm gonna vote for Ms. Heine on the next Kisaragi Supreme Leader popularity poll. She's technically a supreme leader. Sure, there's a *former* before her official title, and she was technically on the enemy side when she held it, but still."

"Me too, me too."

"Actually, I'm told she's a Kisaragi slave. Does that mean we can do pervy things to her?"

"No, we're not allowed to do pervy things to slaves on this planet."

"A slave we can't do pervy things to isn't a slave at all! Why didn't we just take Ms. Heine as a prisoner of war?! We could've done whatever we wanted under the guise of interrogation!"

"Six, you idiot! You stupid, useless moron! You could've handled things way better!"

The peons rattle off complaints without a second thought.

"It's not my fault. It's all Lady Lilith's doing. The reason everything's so chaotic is because the old Demon Lord died thanks to her carelessness."

"I'm definitely putting in a negative score for Lady Lilith in the next poll."

"Me too, me too."

"You're all starting to get on my nerves. If you're just going to get in the way, then leave! I'm trying to take my work seriously!"

Heine finally loses her cool, but here comes Viper with snacks.

"Wh-what's wrong, Heine? What's going on here...?"

Seeing the row of Combat Agents sitting down, Viper tilts her head curiously.

"Lady Viper, they've come to slack off and ogle me! That white-haired woman is even charging admission...!"

Heine begins complaining to Viper, but Snow simply snorts.

"Hmph, what's wrong with making a show of demons who lost the war? The money that your behind brings in will go toward donations for the war victims. You're not actually complaining about that, are you?"

It's a pretty ridiculous way of phrasing it, but I guess Heine feels a bit guilty about the lack of reparations, and she bites back her retorts. Snow's words may sound noble, but I know what she's really thinking. She's probably going to call herself a victim of war by citing the loss of her magic swords, and she'll pocket all the money.

But just as I think this, something unexpected happens.

"...I see, I see. In that case, I'll take my clothes off and put on a show in Heine's stead. Then you can distribute the money you make to the victims—"

"What the—?! Vi! Hey, Vi!"

Without missing a beat, Viper begins undoing the buttons of her top.

"Lady Viper, please don't believe this white-haired woman's words! ...Hey!"

"Ms. Snow's run off with the money!" yells one of the agents.

"I guess she freaked out because the situation started getting dicey! Someone call Alice! We'll tell her everything!" says another.

?? month/?? day

Since any further interruptions will slow down the hunt for the Sand King, Rose, now healed, has been assigned to guard Heine.

By that, I mean Rose is also breathing fire on the boiler to speed things up.

Now that Heine's come up with the idea of fencing herself off, there's nothing to see.

As for me, I still don't have access to my allowance, so I'm effectively grounded.

I guess I could go gather some mipyokopyoko eggs like Snow was doing the other day.

Grimm, the only other person who could treat me to a night out, is still dead.

Mr. Destroyer's batteries are currently around 80 percent full.

It can move around fine as is, but due to the designer's intent, Mr. Destroyer's power level changes depending on its charge. Our preference is to have it fight at about 120 percent.

Heine continues producing flames day in, day out, while Viper and I start making progress on that terrible game. And just as we advance into the final levels...

...Mr. Destroyer finishes charging.

[Status Report]

The expansion of Hideout City is progressing smoothly.

Recently, we've completed a water-treatment facility and a power plant, and our quality of life continues to improve.

It's nice that both facilities are very eco-friendly and low-cost.

Mr. Destroyer's done charging, so we'll be attempting to defeat the Sand King tomorrow.

A Heine Fund has been established and will be distributed to the war victims.

At Alice's urging, we've also started a Snow Fund, but it hasn't done brought in much money. I guess the gap in model quality is too great.

Also, using Fermat's Last Theorem as a solution to a game puzzle is cruel.

Vi spent hours puzzling over it, only to have Alice solve it right before her eyes. It took a long time for her to stop apologizing and calling herself useless.

All right, I'll send another report after we've defeated the Sand King.

Reporting Agent:

Combat Agent Six

A Celebration of Villainy

1

Sitting in the wastelands near the hideout, Mr. Destroyer is extremely conspicuous.

This is where we plan to fight the Sand King.

We've set traps all over the place in hopes of slowing it down, and in the middle of our traps is the bait Alice whipped up herself.

"Boss, can I have a little of that?"

"That's the bait for the Sand King. If you eat everything you come across, you'll get sick."

Rose gazes longingly at the bait set out on the ground.

Since it's all-hands-on-deck, everyone who can fight—minus Grimm, for obvious reasons—is out here.

...Feeling pity for the ravenous Rose, Viper pulls out a snack.

"Mr. Six gave me something called Calorie-Z. Would you like—?"

"Don't mind if I do!"

Before Viper finishes speaking, Rose grabs the supplement bar.

She seems to have grown attached to Viper and usually falls asleep in her presence.

Maybe Demon Lords give off a scent that Chimeras love or something.

For some reason, Heine shoots a nasty look at the traps we've set.

"...Hey, Six. Back when we attacked the castle, my sorcerer stone exploded right in front of me. Did *you* set that trap?"

"...? I don't remember doing anything like that."

"Huh? O-oh, I see. It doesn't seem like you're lying, s-so sorry for suspecting you..."

Heine apologizes, but she still seems a little skeptical of me.

Alice glances over at me as though examining some unusual animal.

"Hey, Alice, could you stop looking at me like that?"

"...Oh, sorry. I was just wondering what your memory capacity is like."

I ignore Alice's strange remark and confirm the placement of the traps along the plain.

The wire traps are designed to immediately bind anyone stepping on their triggers.

Alice nods in approval as she surveys them.

"The bait's designed for carnivores this time. This should draw the Sand King to—"

Before Alice finishes her sentence, we hear a loud crash.

Looking in the direction of the noise, we notice the bait successfully lured in its first carnivore. Tiger Man has been snared.

"Well done, Alice! This trap should definitely work on the Sand King. It certainly drew Tiger Man's attention."

"Do you want to get your ass kicked that badly, Tiger Man? Someone get this waste of oxygen out of here!"

As Tiger Man, bound from head to toe, mewls in distress, Alice crosses her arms and yells:

"I've explained the plan several times, but since I'm worried that some of you still don't have any idea what's going on, I'm going over it one more time!"

I nod repeatedly in agreement.

Your average Combat Agent is as dumb as a box of rocks, so multiple explanations are a must.

"When the Sand King emerges from its hole, the Combat Agents will fill in the hole with quick-drying cement while it's distracted by the bait. Tiger Man, Rose, Viper, Heine—the four of you will defend the agents as they work. Then, once the Sand King's escape route's cut off, you can leave the rest to me."

I'd forgotten most of the plan up to this point, but I notice something when it's explained again.

"Hey, Alice, I didn't hear you mention my name."

"You're a Combat Agent, aren't you? You'll be helping with the cement."

......

"Wait, that's work for the expendables! I wanna do something more important! Something that'll win me a bunch of accolades!"

Hearing my words, Snow also pleads with Alice.

"Alice, I didn't hear my name, either! Please, I can't go back to Tillis without any major achievements...!"

"Your specs are on par with an above-average human's at best. I don't care what you do. Just try not to die. If you kick the bucket, Tillis will probably use that as leverage to negotiate new terms."

"I've known you for a long time, you know... Can't you at least *pretend* to care about me...? Oh, forget it! Defending is the Royal Guard's specialty, so I'll play defense! I'll watch over the whole battlefield from here, then reinforce whichever place is in trouble!" says Snow, pouting.

Once everyone is in position, I stand with my arms crossed and try to look important. Again, Alice glances at me as if observing a strange animal.

"…You know, I'm still technically the branch manager and your partner. Why are you looking at me like that?"

"…Well, I've known you for a long time, but I still can't predict how you'll behave. It's fine, though. Do what you want. When I let you run wild, you sometimes produce unexpected results."

Having received Alice's blessing, I turn and call out to those in position.

"The fates of Vi and the demons rest on this battle! Make sure to give it your all!"

"You're one to talk! Hurry on over and get ready!"

As I cockily cheer them on, one of my colleagues seems to have realized something and speaks up.

"…Ohhh. His Evil Points are still in the red, so he can't afford to order any quick-drying cement."

"……   ……"

I can't offer a response because they've seen right through me.

"Laaame! So he can't even fight because of a reason like that?! Ha!"

"Ah-ha-ha-ha-ha-ha-ha! Just go ahead and watch from over there, *Mr. Branch Manager*!"

"If you ask nicely, I might be willing to get you some cement!"

As the expendables start taunting me, I decide on one thing.

"All right, I'm going to kill them during the battle and make it look like an accident."

"Why are you agents always at each other's throats? Is it because you see things in one another that you don't like about yourselves?"

While arguing with the other agents, I feel a tremor beneath my feet, so I scoop up Alice and hop to the side.

Just then, the ground swells.

"Squeesqueesqueee!"

A wild Sand King appears!

2

Alice shouts out as I put her back on the ground:

"Execute—!"

I didn't expect it to appear right under our feet, so the first thing to do is to get clear.

Alice and I maintain our readiness and slowly open some distance between ourselves and the Sand King.

"Hey, Alice, don't shout too loudly. This thing's got good hearing, right? You're fragile. It'd take you out in a single blow. Be careful."

"If that happened, it wouldn't escape with its life. My reactor will blow, and I'll take it out with me."

Your reactor blowing is exactly what I'm worried about!

"Squeesqueesqueeek…"

The Sand King twitches its nose and turns to the bait.

I'm sure it can hear our voices, but it seems fixated on the bait for now.

"Hey, Alice, Tiger Man's still stuck in one of the traps."

"We can just leave him as live bait for the Sand King. It's his own damned fault."

The ruthless android then heads off toward Mr. Destroyer.

As Tiger Man pleads for help, Viper rushes to his aid.

Seeing that, everyone else remembers their roles and leaps into action.

After making it to Tiger Man's side, Viper quickly removes the wires holding him down.

"Lady Viper! Behind you!"

As though answering Heine's voice, Viper lets loose with a punch as she turns around.

"Demon Lord Punch!"

"Squee?!"

Buffeted by an enormous shockwave, the Sand King lets out a short squeal and falls over.

So that's the Demon Lord Punch that's not a kick. First time I've seen it.

"Well done, Vipurr! Leave the rrrrest to me!"

With most of the wires undone, Tiger Man is able to free himself, and after standing up, he cracks the joints in his neck.

It's faintly irritating that I'm still counting on him when he got himself into trouble in the first place.

Speaking of, it seems like the Sand King has identified our traps and is purposefully avoiding them.

Which means Tiger Man tripped a trap that even a mole can avoid.

…While all this is going on, the agents who've arrived at the Sand King's hole start pouring quick-drying cement into it.

"The Sand King's coming this way!" One of my colleagues pouring concrete shouts out a warning.

Seems the Sand King, realizing it's a trap, is trying to run.

…However.

"Nope! I'm not letting you pass! If you wanna get by, you'll have to leave something valuable! Don't think you'rrre getting away fur frrreeeee!"

"I'll reduce you to ashes with my flames! Your death will be anything but quick!"

"Listening to you two makes me feel like we're doing something bad…"

The three fighters assume a battle formation around the Sand King.

After Heine halts its movements with her flames, Tiger Man quickly closes the distance.

"Grrrrraaaah!"

"Squeesqueesquee!"

The Sand King and Tiger Man, each well aware of the other's strength, exchange cautious glances.

Then Rose, who ducked behind Tiger Man, uses him as a springboard to leap into the air.

"Bow before my lightning!"

Rose yells something as she latches onto the Sand King.

"Sleep for all eternity! Blue Lightning!"

Her horn glows bluish-white, and she discharges electricity from her body.

Evidently, the Sand King's never encountered an electrical attack before and, twitching, hurriedly swats Rose away.

I lend the swatted Rose a hand.

"Rose, when did you learn a new move?"

"Ms. Alice said, *'I'll feed you some gourmet food,'* and gave me something called an *unagi don*. Ever since then, I've been able to do this zappy thing."

Where I'm from, *unagi don*, a dish of eel over rice, is pretty gourmet if you ask me. I have a feeling that Alice used a special kind of eel to make this one, though…

As I help Rose up, Tiger Man and Heine unload on the visibly weakened Sand King.

"Looks like it's numb frrrrom the shock and can't move rrright!"

"This is great! Time to turn it into barbecue!"

The Sand King tries to retreat in the face of the two warriors' onslaught.

Its escape hole is being blocked by Tiger Man and Heine, though, and behind them, the agents are filling it up.

Understanding it can't retreat, the Sand King gets up on its hind legs.

Just seeing the giant claws, which can tear through tough power armor like paper, is enough to dispel any illusions that this'll be an easy fight.

"…Daaaamn. It rrrreally is big…"

"O-our job is to defend the hole and the agents, right? We can leave fighting this thing to the ones in the back, right…?"

As the two look up in shock at the building-size monster, we receive an answer to Heine's question.

"Yep, well done, everyone. Looks like the hole's plugged, so leave the rest to me."

*   *   *

Hearing Alice's voice from the speaker system, we hear the low-rumbling engine noise that every Kisaragi employee knows all too well.

Mr. Destroyer, the Multilegged Combat Vehicle, steps out in front of the Sand King.

The beast's escape route is cut off, and it's surrounded by enemies looking to take it out once and for all.

"Squeesqueesquee, squeeeek!"

The Sand King lets out a high-pitched series of squeaks.

"Yeah, well, bring it, you damned mole! Monster-slaying isn't just for Heroes!"

Mr. Destroyer and the Sand King finally face off in earnest...

"Taste the power of science!"

"Squeeee!"

Far from Hideout City, they engage in a genuine giant-monster battle.

3

Having returned to the base, we first decide to wash Mr. Destroyer, who did the most work today.

"Mr. Destroyer really is the best. A mere mole is no match for it."

Alice, a firm believer in science and nothing else, happily pats Mr. Destroyer's hull.

The Sand King, which had long plagued the demons as well as the neighboring country, was finally put down after a fierce duel with Mr. Destroyer.

Despite its adorable appearance, it was still a great monster, and it put up a hell of a fight until the very end. Mr. Destroyer is a true asset for allowing us to take care of that monster.

"Mr. Destroyer's damaged all over now. The least I can do is fill the cracks with grains of rice."

"What the hell are you trying to do to Mr. Destroyer?! Do you *want* to die?! I'll fix the damage myself. It'll take some time, but my repairs will be so thorough that, by the time I'm done, you'll be able to see your reflection in the hull."

Alice has an attachment to Mr. Destroyer bordering on obsession. She forces us to also treat it like a person in conversation, but I suppose that attachment stems from it being a fellow robot.

...Heine, who has been oddly quiet since the end of the battle between the Sand King and Mr. Destroyer, bows her head deeply.

"Mr. Destroyer, was it? Thank you so very much for taking down the Sand King. Usually, you don't move at all, and I thought you were just lazy, but I was wrong. I thank you, from the bottom of my heart, for accomplishing the long-held hope of demonkind."

Heine then deeply bows her head to Mr. Destroyer. It seems like she's got a strange misunderstanding of what it actually is.

Oh, right, she wasn't there for the fight between Mr. Destroyer and Russell's giant robot.

Just when I try to tell her that Mr. Destroyer is similar to a golem...

"Mr. Destroyer says the power you generated is the reason he was able to defeat the Sand King. The electricity you helped create with your high-quality flames was most delicious."

"R-really?! I see. My flames helped..."

Alice begins pumping the ignorant Heine's head full of weird ideas, but every Kisaragi operative other than me is already busy preparing the victory party.

Which is why Alice, Heine, and I are the only ones here.

I opt to jump on Alice's bandwagon.

"Mr. Destroyer is our trump card, and he usually spends his days sleeping as a result. The harder you work in the power plant, Heine, the stronger Mr. Destroyer becomes."

"Is that true?! ...Okay then! From now, I'll redouble my efforts!"

"Very good. Mr. Destroyer is looking forward to your help, but he doesn't want you to work too hard. He's asking that I give you some time off as I promised before."

Tears spill from Heine's eyes.

"Oh, Mr. Destroyer..."

Looks like she's just as thickheaded as me and Rose.

I've been hearing announcements of Evil Point gains throughout our entire conversation with Heine, and at this rate, it looks like I'll be in the black again soon.

As we continue teasing her, Viper shows up.

"Um, I was told preparations for the party are complete, so I came to collect you all..."

"Oh, gotcha. Once Mr. Destroyer's clean, we'll head over."

Hearing that, Heine smiles and offers her help.

"I'll help, too! It looks like Mr. Destroyer fell asleep. When he wakes up, I'm sure he'll be surprised by how clean we made him!"

"Huh...? Um, what's Heine talking about...?"

Clearly understanding Mr. Destroyer isn't a living being, Viper looks confused by Heine's words.

"In commemoration of the Kisaragi Corporation's defeat of the Sand King, I'd like to begin with a short—"

With the microphone in one hand, I'm about to start my lead-in to the toast at the party grounds constructed in Hideout City...

"Get on with it!"

"We wanna drink already! Skip the speech and get to the toast!"

The expendables heckle me without fear.

I suppose it's about time to make some things clear to them.

"Okay, okay, shut up already! Here's a toast to the rare feat of all you weak-ass, dime-a-dozen agents surviving the battle with the Sand King... Cheers!"

"Cheers…my ass! We're not dime-a-dozen!"

With that half-assed toast, a wave of clinking glass washes over our group.

We've turned Hideout City square into a party venue, setting up several tables for a buffet-style gathering.

The newly immigrated demon residents have joined us for the toast.

With the Sand King gone, they'll now formally become residents of this city.

Meaning now's a good time to get to know them better.

But still…

"There's a succubus! A real-life succubus! And I bet that girl with the pointy fang is a vampire! Damn, this planet is paradise! I'm so happy!"

"More like a furry paradise… There's so many fluffy people…!"

"I heard the kingdom of Grace was short on men thanks to the war, but it looks like the demons are in a pretty similar situation in terms of gender ratio… I think I'm gonna like it here…"

Seeing how the agents are eyeing the demons, it doesn't seem like they'll need my help making new friends.

The folks on the demon side have surrounded Tiger Man and are offering him praise after watching him fight.

"You're Tiger Man, yes? I hear you stood resolutely in front of the Sand King to keep it from escaping!"

"Tiger Man, you're so dreamy! I just love your rugged chest hair… Can I touch it?"

"Sir Tiger Man, if you would spare a moment of your time for us… Ohhh, what a man. Even the charms of a succubus won't work on him… So this is what a hero is made of…"

The succubi press their chests up against him, but Tiger Man offers no reaction, gulping down the rest of the beer in his mug.

Unused to this sort of reaction, the more they're ignored, the harder the demonesses try to get his attention…

Rose (predator) and an orc (prey) sit side by side and devour their food. The Lilim girl Camille wanders by to give her thanks, and Tiger Man follows her every movement with an intense gaze.

I'm stuffing my face, enjoying the chaotic atmosphere of the party, when Viper comes over to me.

"Mr. Six, thank you so much for everything. It's thanks to you all that the demons have managed to smile again. We were invaders, and yet... How can we ever repay you...?"

As Viper goes through her spiel again, I wave the piece of meat I've been eating at her.

"Vi, you're always so formal. You just need to say something like, *Thanks, I look forward to working with you from here on out*, and leave it at that. We Combat Agents are really only good for fighting, so we might not have a lot to do most of the time. When I have downtime, though, I'd love it if you helped me with video games again. Sound good?"

"Yes, I'd be happy to! ...Um, oh...that is..."

Viper replies eagerly but then seems at a loss for words.

...Oh, right. I'm going to have a bit of free time now that the Sand King's gone, but I guess people like Viper, who are actually good at paperwork, will find themselves even busier from now on.

"Oh, right, I understand. Vi, you're gonna be the most in-demand person in the hideout, after all. But you still owe me, so I won't forgive you if you just forget about it. At the very least, I'll have you help me finish this stupid game we've been playing. That's something I won't budge on as the branch manager."

At my selfish request, Viper looks a little happy and a little sad...

"Very well. So you still need my help to finish the game..."

"Yes, it's a promise. A promise is binding! I easily forget promises that don't benefit me, but I never forget promises like this one."

Just then.

"There's no need to thank him, Viper. He didn't do anything in the fight against the Sand King."

Despite being unable to hold her liquor, Snow interrupts our conversation, glass in hand...

"I did contribute! When the Sand King showed up, I protected Alice! Besides, you didn't do anything, either! All that talk at the start, and you're nowhere to be found during the fight!"

"Silence! That very subject is why I'm here! ...Remember, I was close by when the Sand King appeared, was I not?"

Snow says this quietly, as though in a whisper.

"I was caught off guard at the time. And well..."

...?

"Oh! Hold on... When the Sand King made its dramatic entrance, did you get caught up in the blast and pass out?!"

"Shhh, don't say that so loudly! Others might hear us! A-anyway, I can't face Her Highness like this. In the worst-case scenario, I might be dismissed from her service..."

......

"So you want me to let you take credit for saving Alice? I'm desperate for glory this time, too! Don't eat off my plate!"

"Please...! If I get fired and have nowhere to go, could I possibly... you know...like Rose and Grimm...?"

What about Rose and Grimm?

I hope she's not begging me to marry and support her like Grimm always is.

Backed into a corner, Snow glares at me.

"Why can you never take a hint?! Or are you really just that stupid?! Anyone else would've figured out what I'm getting at by now!"

"What the hell are you talking about?! Why are you yelling at me?"

"Why do you two always get into a shouting match the moment you see each other?! Can't we all just get along?!"

Viper hurriedly tries to insert herself between us, but Combat Agents are pretty much all thugs, Snow notwithstanding. This squabbling's just our regular form of communication.

"I'll forgive you today for Vi's sake, but you won't be so lucky next time!"

"Th-there are times when I really envy you. I think of just how blissfully easy it would be to say what I want, do what I want, and live life as I please..."

Viper lets out a sigh of relief as we bury the hatchet for the moment.

"Vi, you're always so tense. Try to relax a little. Here, I'll lend you the video game, so play it when you want to slack off from work." I hand the portable console to Viper.

She doesn't have to be totally useless like us, but I do think this girl should take it easy every now and then.

"N-no, I don't think it's good to skip work... But okay, I'll borrow it for a bit. I'll return it in a week or so..."

"Only a week? You can keep it forever if you'd like. I mean, I plan to come see you in the office every day anyway."

Having taken that awful game into her hands, Viper smiles as she bows her head in thanks.

"One week will be plenty... Thank you for everything, Mr. Six."

As Viper happily cradles the game to her chest, I can't help but feel uneasy.

I feel like I just caught a glimpse of what they call a "death flag."

"Hey, Vi..."

"Oh, Viper, there you are."

Alice appears before I can say anything. If she's here, I guess Heine fully took over the task of cleaning and shining Mr. Destroyer.

"Ms. Alice, is it time?"

"Yeah, it's time. All right, let's get going. Snow, you're coming with us."

Time for what?

When I try to go with them, Viper stops me.

"I have a few things left to take care of, so please wait here, Mr. Six."

Oh, I guess she's finishing the last of the paperwork for today.

Snow's probably going with them because she was useless in the fight, and they're making her help to make up for it.

"All right then, Vi, see you tomorrow."

As I call out to her, Viper briefly turns back to glance at me.

"...Yes, see you tomorrow."

She furrows her brow a moment, and her smile seems forced.

As I watch her delicate form recede, I think back to what she said when she took the game from me.

"One week will be plenty... Thank you for everything, Mr. Six."

I wonder she didn't just say *thank you*.

Why did she make it feel like that was the last time she'd speak to me?

I decide to ask her about it when she's done with her work for the day, but...

...after leaving with Alice, Viper never returns to the hideout.

The announcement that the kingdom of Grace would celebrate the defeat of the Sand King by executing the Demon Lord came the next day.

4

As I pace around the office, Rose, tucked under a blanket on the sofa, speaks up.

"Boss, calm down, please. Let's just wait until Ms. Alice can explain the details."

"Alice hasn't come back, either. And what the hell are you doing? Whose blanket is that?"

Apparently, when Alice and Viper left yesterday, they were heading to the castle in the kingdom of Grace.

This morning, the news of the Defeat of the Sand King Celebration and the Demon Lord's execution came out, but...

"This is Viper's blanket that I won from Russell in a fight. I find it soothing to have it wrapped around me."

The two Chimeras, who are quite attached to Viper, have also been on pins and needles all morning.

Heine, the one most negatively affected by the news, has holed herself up in the power plant and is obsessively generating electricity.

No doubt she plans to ask Mr. Destroyer, currently recharging next to the facility, for help.

Then again, Heine seemed to have known something like this would happen from the time she was locked up in the dungeon of the Demon Lord's Castle.

She might be trying to distract herself by focusing on her work.

"You probably don't remember because you were asleep, but when we first met Vi, she said she wanted the kingdom of Grace to execute her as recompense for the demons' many transgressions. She probably means to take responsibility for the entire war, but I didn't realize she was this serious about it."

Viper had been working hard every day, approaching her tasks with the utmost care and focus, but I guess she was putting in her best effort because she planned to die from the very beginning.

...Just then, the door to the office opens, and Tiger Man pokes his head in.

"Six, come with me. Emergency meeting in the cafeteria."

I can tell Tiger Man isn't messing around because, once again, he's forgotten to purr.

"I take it you guys have hearrrrd the news? Man, as soon as we killed the Sand King, things got weirrrd," says Tiger Man, surrounded by Kisaragi agents.

"Why are they executing Ms. Viper? Do those Grace Kingdom

assholes not understand just how valuable attractive young women are?!"

"Viper's such a good girl. She's beautiful but in possession of a kindness and a common sense you'd never find at Kisaragi..."

"Well, she might not have *thaaat* much common sense. I mean, the other day when I said, *'Heh-heh-heh, so, young lady, what color panties are you wearing?'* as a greeting, she tried to answer me normally."

The last agent to speak up gets smacked by everyone in attendance.

Russell, who's been stirring a pot in the kitchen, says with a note of exasperation:

"Will you calm down, guys? We have no idea what's going on until Alice gives us the details. There's time until the execution. So right now, we should wait on Alice."

"Mr. Russell, you need to calm down, too. You've been stirring the pot for a while now, but you forgot to put in any ingredients."

Russell falls silent at Rose's words.

I take the opportunity to get up on a table and shout:

"Alice hasn't come back, either, dammit! This is a challenge to us by the kingdom of Grace! Vi is *our* prisoner of war, so why should we sit back and let the kingdom of Grace execute her?! Beautiful young women are valuable assets! If they're planning to take one of our assets, that's no different than a declaration of war!"

"Wow, I actually agree with something Six said, for once! Yeah, we're an evil organization! If there's something we want, we should just take it!"

"Heh-heh-heh, now we're talking like a real evil organization. We've all been behaving ourselves ever since we got to this rock. Now's the time to do some real damage...!"

The Combat Agents, who are all petty thugs at heart, cheer in agreement.

The rest depends on the influential mutant Tiger Man's opinion, but...

"If Vipurr is gone, no matter how grrrrreat a sorcerer stone I obtain, no one else can make me a kid again! If the possibility isn't zerrrro, I'm not giving up!"

I don't understand what he's saying, nor do I want to understand, but if nothing else, he seems to agree we have to rescue Viper.

"Ugh, you people really are dumb. Since I'm afraid you'll mess up on your own, I, Russell of the Water, will lend you a hand. I feel like you all have been underestimating me lately. I'll show those pitiful humans of the kingdom of Grace just what I'm capable of."

"Mr. Russell, you just uttered one of the Kisaragi manual's forbidden lines. If you come with us, you'll probably die, so just stay here and cook something."

I guess everyone agrees we have to rescue Viper.

"All right then, let's get to it! Prepare for war! Remember Kisaragi's real nature! We're gonna invade the kingdom of Grace and get Alice and Vi back!"

"""""Yaaaaahoooo!"""""

And just as we all get fired up...

"You morons. Why the hell would you want to invade the kingdom of Grace? They don't have much in the way of resources. The place to invade is *Toris*, you hear me? Toris."

Having returned while we weren't paying attention, Alice speaks to us from the doorway.

"So why are you doing the walk of shame despite being an android, huh? Also, the reason we're gonna invade the kingdom of Grace is to save Vi. We don't want to take over the country itself!"

"That's why I'm telling you to stop. Viper's execution was decided from the start. It was included in the terms when they agreed to let the demons settle in Hideout City if the Sand King was defeated. We discussed this with Tillis herself."

Well, I suppose that's what I should expect from a cold, calculating android. She's completely heartless.

"Hey, Alice, doesn't Vi's presence help you as well? I mean, you were piling all sorts of work on her. Given how clever you are, surely you've got some way of saving her, right?"

"It's true that since Kisaragi's full of idiots, having Viper was helpful. But to end a war, there needs to be a scapegoat who can take all the blame. And given that's what Viper wants, the rest of us aren't in any position to stop her."

...True, given how seriously self-sacrificial Viper is, that's something she'd probably say.

But...

"I hate to do this, but I'm invoking my wartime command authority. Forget about Viper. We finally got everything settled. Don't mess it up. This is for Kisaragi."

At Alice's unusually stern warning, everyone present falls silent.

It's now morning, five days before the Defeat of the Sand King Celebration.

Grimm's voice rings out in the training grounds next to the hideout.

"Understand me, Commander. I'm not such an easy woman that I'll forget everything just because you take me on a date!"

The day after we're lectured by Alice, Grimm is fuming. Apparently, she's upset that we didn't even notice she came back to life at some point.

"Look, it's not our fault. You're usually dead when we need you. I mean, for the Sand King battle, if we'd had you around, we would've had a much easier time."

Learning she missed out on the battle with the Sand King, especially after missing the Demon Lord's Army battle, is a heavy blow to Grimm.

"...I won't be swayed by sweet words like *if we'd had you around*...
But I made you lunch. Would you like it?"

I take the bento box from the easily swayed Grimm.

"Let's go on a date and eat it together."

Hearing that, Grimm curls her lips into a poorly concealed smile.

"Yes, I suppose enjoying a packed lunch together is a regular part
of a date. Um, Commander, can you say the words *let's go on a date*
again? One hundred more times, perhaps?"

"N-no way...!"

Seeing how happy she is just to hear the word *date* makes me feel
guilty considering where I'm taking her...

"I can't believe I fell for something like this again! I should've
known you only invited me out on a whim! It was the first time anyone
had asked me out on a date, too! Give me back my first time!"

We're near the woods that spread out in front of the hideout.

"What are you talking about? This is a proper date. Have you
never heard of picnics?"

"Hold on! I can understand calling it a picnic if we're out picking
berries or wildflowers. But this is in no way a picnic!"

Currently, Grimm and I are gathering mipyokopyoko eggs.

Since I heard an amateur can't tell the difference between mupyokopyoko and mipyokopyoko eggs, I invited Grimm, who seemed to
have nothing else to do.

"Besides, why did you invite me of all people? I'm not an out-
doorsy type! Snow knows how to tell the difference, too!"

It's true that pushing a wheelchair through these woods is a bit of
a hassle...

"Snow hasn't come back from the castle, and I thought you'd know
a lot about things like this."

"...Well, sure, I do use monster components as part of my job sometimes, but... *Sigh*, okay, just this once, all right? But in exchange, you need to help me gather materials to use in my rituals."

Well, I guess I can help with that.

...And lo, there's some right there.

"Hey, Grimm, which pyokopyoko's eggs are these?"

"These are mipyokopyoko eggs. A strong shock will make them explode, so mind how you handle them... I heard you're short on money since Alice cut off your allowance, but are you so broke that you need to take odds jobs like this?"

"I'm broke enough that I can't go partying in the kingdom these days."

Grimm smiles thinly.

"...Then how about we go drinking tonight? I've heard about that girl Viper. I know you two were close, so I'm sure you're still struggling with that... As the Archbishop of Zenarith, the least I can do is comfort you at a time like this."

"...Okay."

But I'm not going to be comforted.

I'm going because there's something I want to ask Grimm about mipyokopyoko eggs...

Three more days until the celebration.

The demons in Hideout City have started asking us for jobs.

They feel that, because Viper and Heine have been working so hard for their sakes, they can't just sit around doing nothing.

I guess the news about Viper's execution was intentionally kept from them so as not to cause a stir.

With a sudden increase in her paperwork, Alice gets caught grumbling pretty often. She better not look to us for assistance, though. Since we can't read the local language, there's nothing we can do to help.

When I shrug my shoulders and cite that as my excuse, she threatens to print out a bunch of paperwork in Japanese for me to do instead.

I return the favor by telling her it'd just increase her workload because she'll have to go through and correct all the errors Combat Agents would make filling out the forms. She seemed to have a pretty hard time believing we would brag about something like that.

Two days until the celebration.

Lately, Tiger Man's been howling at night, which has been a serious nuisance.

There are even more voices joining the chorus tonight.

Seems they're trying to distract themselves from Viper's absence.

But with three of them howling, it's just way too loud.

Too much yowling is going to attract monsters to Hideout City and the kingdom, too, so I wish they'd stop.

"Tomorrow, there's going to be a huge festival commemorating the defeat of the Sand King. They'll also be conducting *that* ceremony at the end of the festival, but you guys better not intervene."

The day before the victory celebration, Alice comes in to give us one final warning.

It's a bitter pill to swallow, but in wartime, command authority is absolute within Kisaragi.

Everyone here knows that.

An organization can't survive without following its chain of command.

Everyone seems to nod in agreement, and then...

Tonight's the long-awaited Defeat of the Sand King Celebration.

Maybe it's because there's a particularly beautiful moon out, but the three beasts we keep in the hideout are howling again and drawing attention from monsters.

It's possible that predators will be attracted to the city even with a festival underway.

As hired Combat Agents, we must fulfill our duty and defend the kingdom of Grace.

And so driven by that sense of duty...

"We're the Combat Agents of an evil organization! You think we give a damn about rules?! Ha!"

""""Yaaahooo!"""""

This is about par for the course for Kisaragi Combat Agents.

If they wanna throw a celebration so badly, we'll gladly bring the party.

I take out the mask I usually don't wear because it's so stupid-looking and head into the city to witness Viper's last moments.

5

Viper's execution is going to be conducted at around midnight in the city square.

I suppose it's meant to be the grand finale to the festival, but from our outsiders' perspective, it's just a bit of grotesque showmanship.

Having entered the city, we don our masks, completely ignoring the curious stares of the residents.

"Okay, so we're just Combat Agents here in formal attire to enjoy the festivities. And everyone knows there's no way that Kisaragi agents can be around this many people and not cause problems. With that in mind, everything that's about to happen should be seen as nothing but normal, everyday activity."

A group of strange men, wearing a bunch of weird masks, all nod in understanding.

Insubordination is heavily punished, so we all ready our excuses, weak as they are.

"Okay, the ones who'll infiltrate the castle will be me and...

Combat Agent Ten, who only recently got released from the castle's dungeon."

"Sneaking into the castle's as easy as taking an afternoon walk for me now. Leave it to me."

I was wondering why I hadn't seen Combat Agent Ten lately, and it turns out he royally screwed up again and was taken into custody.

"So what did you do this time?"

"Nothing major. Since I'd reflected on why it was wrong of me to sneak into Princess Tillis's room at night, I decided to sneak into her room in broad daylight and have a soak in her bathtub."

There's a lot I want to ask, including why the hell he took a bath in someone else's home without asking, but I guess I can trust him with the task of stealing into the castle (again).

"After the last time I broke in, they revamped the castle's security measures, but…that shouldn't be a problem for me."

Is it really okay to trust this man with anything?

I suddenly find myself worrying, but I'd be lying if I said this guy didn't have a knack for infiltration.

I touch the mask I'm wearing and adjust its fit.

"I know you were locked up all this time, but do you even know where I want to go?"

"Of course I know. When it comes to sneaking into Princess Tillis's room, I'm your man."

Completely missing the point, Ten gives me a thumbs-up.

Maybe I should pick someone else to do this… It's not too late, right…?!

As Ten and I head to the castle…

…I retrieve something from my backpack. I've been taking advantage of moments when the residents aren't looking to toss these onto rooftops that look like they get plenty of moonlight.

"Six, what are those?"

"Mipyokopyoko eggs. They hatch when they absorb enough moonlight."

Yes, what I'm planting are the eggs I collected with Grimm.

Ten, running next to me, nods in understanding even though he doesn't know what's going on.

"So it's like when I tossed my used tissues onto the roofs of the neighboring houses from my second-story window."

"Uh, just to make sure, you used those tissues to blow your nose, right? Don't do that in Hideout City, got it?"

Having finished my egg tossing, I approach the castle's outer wall with Ten.

The walls are even taller now than during my last visit, and all the entrances other than the main gate have been removed.

But for some reason, there's no sign of guards tonight.

It might have something to do with the fact that, for whatever reason, a lot of monsters have been spotted near the city.

"Well, how do we get inside? Let me first note that I want you to take us to the dungeon."

"I know the dungeon like my own backyard. Leave it to me. For infiltration…let's go with this."

That's when Ten produces a couple of maid outfits.

"…Let me guess. We're going to pretend to be maids who work in the castle and waltz in like we belong here."

"Exactly. The walls are designed to make it impossible to climb over them, and with the only entrance—the main gate—shut tight, we need the watchmen to let us in."

Well, I can follow up to that point.

"If you were on watch, who would you stop? A friendly merchant? A person in everyday clothes? The more effort you put into perfecting your disguise, the more likely you'll mess up. In that case, it's best to go the complete opposite route. If a couple of burly men wandered by dressed like maids, you'd do your best to avoid interacting with them, right?"

Well, sure, I wouldn't want to interact with us, but I'm pretty sure we'd definitely get stopped.

Ten begins changing into the maid outfit without any concern for whoever might be watching.

"What do you think? Does it look good?"

"Good enough to make me think this just might work..."

Ten's evolved into such a weird creature that any watchman would probably avoid him like the plague.

"I'll lend you my optical camo. Use that to hide yourself and follow me."

I take the light-refracting camouflage device from Ten and quickly turn it on.

Before me, a buff man dressed in power armor with a maid outfit pulled over it strides confidently into the castle.

The two watchmen, completely taken aback by Ten's appearance, seem to struggle with something internally before pretending nothing's wrong and opening the gate... No, they're totally looking the other way.

I *really* didn't expect this to work.

This man might be more than just your average pervert.

Ten continues walking, never once turning his head as he whispers to me.

"Six, the dungeon is around this next corner. If someone catches me, don't hesitate to leave me behind. I'm going to make my way to Princess Tillis's room. Godspeed," says the outlandish maid, rather dashingly.

I nod, even though I know he can't see me because of the camo.

"Sir Six, I had a feeling you would come."

*   *   *

Tillis, leading a group of knights, is there waiting for me. Snow's standing next to her with a conflicted look on her face.

6

"I gave the watchmen advance notice to let anyone from Kisaragi through, but I didn't expect them to let you through looking like *that*."

She looks a bit uncomfortable when she says this.

"Sir Six, our nation's political climate is such that we simply cannot let bygones be bygones. For the sake of a bright future between our kingdom and Kisaragi, would you mind turning around and going home?"

Tillis is more serious than I've ever seen her before.

...But she's not talking to me. I'm still hidden by optical camo. She's speaking to the strange, masked maid.

I creep past Tillis with my back to the wall and sneak into the dungeon.

Tillis seems to be pretty intent, so I'm not gonna interrupt her. I'll just leave her in Ten's care.

I easily sneak past the sentry and search for the cell containing the person I'm here to find.

And at the very end of the dungeon...

...I see Viper in a cell, sitting primly on the floor, engrossed in the game I gave her.

"Vi... Vi! This is Six, can you hear me?"

When I whisper to her from outside the cell, Viper twitches and looks up.

"I-is that you, Mr. Six? Where are you?"

As Viper glances around her cell, my inner imp can't help himself.

"I'm transmitting my thoughts directly into your mind from far away, Vi... Can you hear me...? Is my voice reaching you...?"

"Yes, I can hear you! Your voice is coming in loud and clear, Mr. Six!"

Viper looks off into the distance, appearing a bit excited.

Rather than following the sound of my voice, she's probably looking in the general direction of the hideout.

"I didn't know you could use magic as well! And magic as powerful as telepathy, no less!"

Oh, Viper, it wouldn't kill you to be a bit less gullible...

"Forget about my secret powers for now. Tell me what's going on, Vi. Why are you gonna be executed?"

Viper puts on a troubled smile.

"I'm sorry, Mr. Six. I lied to you... I wasn't able to keep my promise of staying with you until you finished your game..."

Viper delicately hugs the console to her chest like it's her newborn child. Considering the gloomy atmosphere of the dungeon, it's a pretty heart-wrenching sight.

"So how far did you get in that dumb game I lent you?"

"I was able to handle most of the puzzles, but the fighting was rather difficult, and I ended up getting stuck..."

If she's never played a game before, the combat segments would be hard, I bet.

"It's okay, I'll handle the fighting. You can just worry about the puzzles, Vi."

"...I'm sorry. My execution is scheduled to take place soon. Everything will be over by the time you get here, Mr. Six..."

Even though Hideout City and the kingdom of Grace are technically neighbors, it still takes half a day to get from one to the other.

Since Viper doesn't know I'm right in front of her, the smile on her face wavers further into sadness.

"I really enjoyed the time I spent with you, Mr. Six. All you did was come to the office and play video games, but listening to you let out weird voices or suddenly complain about something— Well, I found your carefree lifestyle heartwarming."

She doesn't think I'll make it in time, so she begins spilling her feelings.

"Oh, I see. Vi, you probably shouldn't say any more. You might end up regretting it."

I warn her for her own sake, but she just quietly shakes her head.

"I won't have any regrets. When I was helping you with your game, that was the only time I wasn't a Demon Lord awaiting execution, but simply Viper, playing with her friend. I really, really appreciate what you—"

If I let her keep going, there won't be any salvaging this.

"Vi, please don't say any more. I'm a Combat Agent for an evil organization. I might use this embarrassing story to make you do ridic-ulous things in the future, you know."

"It's okay. Remember, I told you when we first met that you could do anything you wanted to me. But even after all the time we spent together, no one at Kisaragi troubled me in the slightest."

When she says this, Viper looks a bit more relaxed than usual.

Since she thinks she's about to be executed, she probably thinks there's no harm in joking around.

"It's not over yet, Vi. It's too early to relax. You might end up getting kidnapped and taken to some evildoer's hideout."

"That's fine by me. If I could be of use to them in any way, I wouldn't mind."

Once again, Viper just goes with the flow.

"Girls shouldn't casually go along with every little thing. I prom-ise you'll end up having regrets if you keep that up."

"I assure you, I won't. If only I could see you again, Mr. Six... I would do anything. Even now, as I wait for the end, not being able to remain by your side is my only regret..."

Viper then chuckles, having teased someone for what might have been the first time in her life.

…I see.

"'Anything,' huh? Well, first, let's get you outta here, Vi."

I take off my mask and deactivate my camo. Viper freezes and stares at me, mouth agape.

"What's wrong, Vi? Your face is all red, Vi! I did say you'd regret it if you kept going, didn't I? Hey, Vi, can you tell me how you feel after giving that embarrassing confession right in front of my eyes?"

"…! …!"

Viper, a blushing, trembling mess, glares daggers at me.

"Mr. Six, you're so mean!"

"And, Vi, you're a liar. I won't let you break your promise. I'll say it as many times as I have to. We're going to finish this stupid game. Together."

I'll think about the rest once I've safely kidnapped Viper and taken her to the hideout.

Viper has a troubled look on her face.

"I can't leave this place. For the demons to be forgiven by this kingdom, I need to—"

"I don't care about any of that. I'm a member of an evil organization. Why should I care what happens between the kingdom of Grace and the demons? I'm just gonna kidnap you, Vi."

Yes, it tends to be forgotten a lot, but on a basic level, we're still evil.

Great acts of villainy, like kidnapping beautiful young women, is technically part of our job description.

"B-but if you do that, you'll drive a wedge between Kisaragi and the kingdom! This could result in another war!"

"If that happens, Alice will figure something out. She's smart, unlike me. Besides, our primary goal is *world* domination. The kingdom's gonna be ours eventually. It was always a question of *when*, not *if*."

"...Oh..."

Viper recoils, but the truth is the truth. After all, we're the bad guys.

"B-but even then, your fellow Kisaragi Combat Agents could end up getting dragged into the war! Surely, that's..."

Wait, is this girl serious?

"You mentioned this yourself, Vi. We're always at one another's throats. Heine even said we were more bloodthirsty than genuine demons."

But that's a no-brainer...

"The job of a Combat Agent is to fight. If there's no more war in the world, we'll be out of work."

Viper goes dumb as I say this without a shred of hesitation.

"Besides, I've thought this for a while, but Combat Agents are mostly scum anyway. If we lose a few, it's no skin off my nose."

"That's awful! You shouldn't say such things!"

Viper's a good girl even in situations like this, but we're running out of time.

I produce my vibrating blade and press it against the cell bars.

"N-no, you mustn't, Mr. Six! There are lots of people who'll be in trouble if I escape! ...Oh!"

In no time at all, the first bar is severed.

As I place my blade against the second, Viper tearfully pleads with me.

"Pl-please stop, Mr. Six. The demons' lives are on the line. If you don't stop, I'll get mad. I really will! I'm still a Demon Lord! I'm strong!"

The second bar clatters to the floor, and as I'm working on the third, Viper glares angrily at me through her tears.

She's so adorable.

"I—I hate you... I thought you were a nice person, Mr. Six. But considering what you're doing, I hate you! Please. We're so close to ending things peacefully! You're going to ruin everything!"

The third bar falls.

Knowing she can't threaten me into compliance, Viper tries to sway me with tears. But she's so cute when she cries.

I bring the blade up to the fourth bar, and Viper grabs the dull side.

"Why do you insist on causing so much trouble? We met only recently, and we don't even know each other that well. I made my peace with this outcome long ago. So please... Please..."

Viper turns away in an attempt to hide her tears.

"Vi, Vi."

As I ignore the gloom and call her name cheerfully, she faces me again.

I'm just a teeny, tiny bit stupider than most people. That's why I can't really deal with important matters or handle heavy topics. But there's one thing I know for sure.

No one truly wants to die.

"For now, let's just head back to the base and play that stupid game."

As the fourth bar rolls onto the ground, Viper breaks out sobbing.

7

Carefully cradling the game console, Viper tags along behind me.

"Mr. Six, it's only until we finish this game, all right? After that, I'll have you return me to the kingdom. I'm going to keep my promise, so you have to keep yours, too, Mr. Six."

"I know, I know. I promise, I promise. But, Vi, your eyes are all red."

Viper casts a suspicious gaze my way. After having a good cry inside her cell, she seems to have stopped holding back with me.

How did this unquestioningly naive young woman end up like this?

"Oh, if the game console breaks, we gotta start over, okay? And before we can do that, we'll have to order a new one from my country, so…"

At those words, Viper tightly cradles the console to avoid damaging it.

"If you break the console, Mr. Six, that condition is null and void. A-also, no slacking off and dying on purpose! Please take it seriously!"

That's fine. I can always just overwrite the save data.

Besides, if I explain the situation, I bet Heine and company will just go ahead and destroy the game console on their own.

Once we reach entrance to the dungeon, I peek outside to assess the situation.

…Straining my ears, I can hear Tillis's serious attempts at reasoning with Ten.

"Sir Six, please give up! This is a matter of a formal treaty between Kisaragi and the kingdom of Grace! …Also, Snow! Stop holding back!"

"N-no, Your Highness… I may not be feeling all that up to it, but I'm not holding back…"

Unfortunately, the optical camo only works for one person. Since I have Viper with me, it'll be really hard to sneak out.

However…

"Gah! Dammit, he really is strong!"

"Surround him! He may be a Kisaragi Combat Agent, but he's unarmed! Hold him down!"

"Combat Agent Six…! S-so this is the power of a man who's taken down the Demon Lord's Elite Four…!"

Out of the corner of my eye, "Agent Six" is brawling with some knights while wearing a maid outfit.

As Tillis noted, Snow doesn't seem as sharp as usual.

Could it be that she's holding back, knowing I'm here to break Viper out?

In order to save myself, I hand the optical camo to Viper.

"This is an item that makes you invisible. I'm going to save my maid self. Use that to escape through the gate."

"I-I'll go and ask Princess Tillis to delay the execution for a bit! So please…"

Viper may say that, but Tillis is a true ruler at heart. I can't imagine she'll pity Viper enough to delay the execution given that her kingdom's authority is on the line.

I take out my mask and put it back on, then run over to the other me.

"This is as far as you go!"

"What the—? Reinforcements?!"

As I appear and block the knights in, a murmur of confusion ripples through their group.

"Hey, me, the mission's complete. Let's get the hell outta here."

But the burly maid only shakes his head.

He puts his hand on his mask and—

"Y-you! You're Sir Combat Agent Ten! Someone, check on the Demon Lord! Sir Ten is a decoy! Forget about him! Restrain the new guy and hurry to the dungeon! Securing the Demon Lord is our top priority!"

As Ten reveals himself, sweat beads on Tillis's brow, and she slowly backs away.

Ignoring the watchful gaze of the knights, Ten slowly makes his way to Tillis.

"I have something I still need to do. Move."

"B-but this is the way to my room… May I ask what you intend to do…?"

Tillis is clearly still bit traumatized by Ten's past actions and continues to nervously retreat.

"Nothing important. For now, feel free to think of me as another piece of furniture in your bedroom."

"I don't understand what you're saying."

I don't, either.

"I thought hard about it while I was locked in the dungeon. I've caused a lot of trouble for you, so I should do whatever I can to atone. I need to make myself useful to you somehow."

Okay, I can understand that, at least.

"That's when I came to this conclusion. All I can do is fight. But you have no use for a man who only knows how to fight, right?"

"Actually, I could really use some skilled soldiers…"

Ten pretends not to hear Tillis and takes her hands in his.

"During my time in the dungeon, I practiced being a chair. And not just a chair; I can also become a bed. Rejoice, Princess Tillis, for on occasion, I shall act as your furniture. I'll pretend to be your chair and your bed and quietly watch over you."

"Guards! Capturing this man is your new highest priority!"

Ten leaves one hell of an impression, putting up fierce resistance and drawing the knights away. Thanks to him, I'm nearing the main gate.

Since even the watchmen are off trying to restrain Ten, it shouldn't be too hard to get out of here.

Ten really is something to make even Tillis lose her calm.

As I admire my comrade's efforts, Viper, hidden by the optical camo, taps me on the shoulder.

I reach out just to confirm she's there…

…but I suddenly feel an invisible hand stop mine.

"Hey…! I'm just trying confirm you're here…!"

"I am! Where were you about to touch?"

She's objecting now, but wasn't she willing to let me do as I pleased until recently?

I guess this is a positive development, but maybe I should've done more while I could...

While struggling with that in my mind, I try to push open the gate, but it doesn't budge.

Oh, I guess you need the keys to open it!

The watchmen aren't stupid. If they had to leave their stations for any reason, of course they'd make sure to lock up first.

Just then.

Suddenly, I hear an explosion ringing from the castle, followed by alarm bells.

"Your Highness! That bell indicates a large number of monsters is threatening the city!"

"And the explosions came from *inside* the city! The beasts may already have gotten in..."

The monster-warning bell is probably thanks to the howling of our three beasts.

As for the explosions, the mipyokopyoko eggs must have hatched...

The knights, naturally curious about what's going on in the city, look toward the gate...

...and see me.

"...! Leave Sir Ten...! *Mmph*... Leave Sir Ten for now and capture that Combat Agent over there! Ask him what he was doing in the dungeon. If there's no sign of the Demon Lord, that man should know where she is!"

The gate doesn't look like it'll open, even when I hit it with my enhanced fist.

Okay, I need to calm down.

If Ten and I get apprehended, the knights will head outside to take care of the monsters.

Which means the gate will open...

"Vi, just stay hidden by the gate. They'll eventually open it from the inside, and you'll be able to escape."

But Viper doesn't reply. I get the feeling she's shaking her head.

Then, I hear the shuffle of feet and a deep breath.

Understanding what she's planning to do, I murmur to the empty air:

"Vi, you're weirdly stubborn, but I don't dislike that about you."

Viper sighs. The optical camo can't keep up with her movements and reveals her.

Looking as though she's finally come to terms with something, Viper swings her left fist and cries:

"Demon Lord Punch!"

8

Finally freed from the castle, I'm sweating bullets as we run through the streets of Grace.

"What's wrong, Mr. Six? You're sweating profusely."

Viper expresses concern for me, but an explosion rings out right as she speaks.

<Evil Points Acquired>

Sweet. The influx of points that started a little bit ago hasn't slowed down.

The eggs that I scattered in the hopes that one or two would hatch seem to be yielding a lot more baby monsters than I expected.

From every corner of the city, I hear cries of "Look out, it's a mipyokopyoko!" followed by the sound of explosions.

"...I'm worried that the dregs of the Demon Lord's Army are conducting terror attacks to try and break you out, Vi..."

"N-none of my demons would ever do anything like that! This

chaos is your doing, isn't it, Mr. Six? I'm sure you know exactly what's going on, don't you?!"

Immediately recognizing this is most likely my fault, Viper stops running and looks around.

"…Perhaps I should just return to my execution…"

"It's mipyokopyoko eggs! It's just mipyokopyoko eggs hatching, and the newly hatched and irate ones exploding! Someone told me the explosion of a newborn mipyokpyoko isn't strong enough to kill anyone!"

But as Viper surveys the damage, the knights from the castle gain on us.

"Vi, let's think of our next move while we run!"

"But there's a person pinned under some wooden debris over there!"

Completely ignoring the approaching knights, Viper goes to help the man crying out in pain.

"Vi, you really are a softy! But I don't dislike that about you, either, Vi!"

While I assume a fighting stance, fully prepared to take on the advancing knights…

"My, my. Stopping and helping the injured to earn brownie points. That's just the sort of shallow behavior I would expect from a home-wrecker."

…Grimm appears, a thin smile on her lips and spouting a line better suited for the black-hearted daughter of a noble.

Moving in to block the knights' path, Grimm has a group of Kisaragi agents backing her up. She snaps her fingers to the one pushing her wheelchair.

"…? What is it, Ms. Grimm? I don't know what I'm supposed to do when you go off script."

"You're supposed to say something along the lines of how I, the

Archbishop of Zenarith, am better suited to helping the injured and that a Demon Lord isn't needed here! Then, you're all supposed to laugh at her! Oh, whatever! I'll say it, so just laugh when I do!"

Grimm goes off on an odd tangent as she heads toward the injured man.

Ah, got it. She's acting a bit like a *tsundere*, but I guess this is her own way of trying to help Viper...

"...Hey, why are you just standing around?! Healing the injured is my job! I'm going to help a handsome man who's been incapacitated, and even though he'll fall in love with me at first sight, I'm going to tell him, *I'm sorry, I already have someone to whom I've promised my future.*"

""""""Ha-ha-ha-ha-ha-ha-ha!"""""""

"Hold on! You're not supposed to laugh at that part! ...Oh, whatever."

...Nope. She probably just wants to flirt with a handsome, helpless man.

Wait, when she mentioned the person she promised her future to, she wasn't talking about me, right? Surely, she hasn't been editing the promise in her mind, right?

Grimm tends to the injured man with all the speed and efficiency of a crazed spinster who's relentlessly practiced for this exact scenario.

"Thank you so much! I really appreciate it!"

Having seen that, Viper shouts a thanks as she dashes off. The knights try to circle around Grimm as she blocks the road.

But the Combat Agents stand in their way...

"H-hold it! Don't let her escape! ...Do you have any idea what you've just done?!"

"Lady Grimm, we can't have you interfering in our activities! Do you not know who that woman is?!"

In response, Grimm smiles seductively and makes a come-hither gesture to the barking knights.

"I'm far more attractive than that fragile girl, wouldn't you say? There's a lovely moon out tonight, so why not have a drink with me, hmm? Just forget about work and—"

Two of the knights turn on their heels.

"We don't have time for this! Men, go around them!"

"There's a back alley behind that street. Let's take that route!"

"……"

Having been completely ignored, Grimm covers her face and trembles.

"Uhhh, Ms. Grimm! I-it's all right, Ms. Grimm, you're a beautiful woman! Six said so himself!"

"Hey, Ms. Grimm's crying for real! What sort of men are you?!"

"Apologize to Ms. Grimm! …Um, Ms. Grimm! I currently have someone I like, so maybe if we're reincarnated and meet each other in the next life, we can date then!"

As those and other such phrases recede into the background, Viper and I turn onto a busy street with a lot of people on it.

It looks like mipyokopyokos aren't the only ones rampaging through the city. Combat Agents are raising hell, too, and I can hear familiar taunts coming from every direction.

But tonight is the Defeat of the Sand King Celebration. A festival isn't complete without a brawl or two. That's just how it is.

Eventually, Viper and I arrive at the square, hearing the screams of Grimm and the knights all the while.

If we can make it to the crowd of people, the knights will probably be at a loss.

After all, they can't very well go around shoving their own citizens.

I, of course, don't hesitate. I am, after all, part of an evil organization.

…Then, as we enter the square, we realize we've been had.

"We've been waiting for you, Sir Six. You've really done it this time…"

A knight commander is there waiting for me, backed by soldiers. The face looks familiar, but the name escapes me. The soldiers all have nets and ropes in their hands, and I can see they're not planning to kill us.

There are over a hundred knights and soldiers present. Taking them all out would be a pretty tall order, even for me.

As I stop and take a deep breath, Viper stands up and hands me the game console she's been cradling this whole time.

"I've solved as many puzzles as I was able to... Um, it's a pity I won't be able to keep my promise, but it's been a long time since I've run this much. It was very refreshing."

Viper then makes a smile free of regret.

"You know, Vi, you seem perfect at a glance, but your weakness is that you give up too easily. I get it. You're brilliant, but you always make a snap decision after weighing the pros and cons for only a few seconds."

I collect myself and open my wrist device for the first time in a long while.

After checking the screen, I show it to Viper.

"Do you know what this number represents, Vi? This is one of the biggest point totals I've ever been able to gather. And this number can directly translate into my power."

I was already about to get out of the red, but after tonight's rampage, my Evil Point total is about to hit quadruple digits.

"N-no, you can't, Mr. Six. I don't want to live at someone else's expense. I don't know what you're planning, but..."

At my fearless grin, the soldiers around me back up.

Yes, the people here are just soldiers who, while I know their faces, I don't know well enough to remember their names.

Which means they've also seen us Combat Agents fight...

"It's okay, Vi. I'll use nonlethal methods to take them out. Sure, they might get a little singed, or blown up, or electrocuted, or frozen, but I promise they won't die."

"No! Please, can't we have a peaceful chat with them, Mr. Six? I won't run away again, so maybe we can negotiate for more time to finish that game…"

At Viper's panicked expression, the knights and soldiers here seem to have figured out my intentions.

I'm definitely in the black again, but I'm more than happy to go back into the red for her.

If I just let Viper die, I'll probably regret it for the rest of my life…

"You've really done it this time, you moron. I told you to stay put, but *nooo*. You couldn't even trust your own partner, huh?"

As I'm deciding which nonlethal weapons to employ, the person I least want to see right now shows up with Tillis and Snow in tow.

"Sorry, Alice, I need you to back down this time. Otherwise, I'm gonna use my points to turn this kingdom into a sea of flames."

"Oh? Is that how you want to play? All right then, give it your best shot. Even if you do manage to take me out, my generator will detonate, and this kingdom, as well as every neighboring nation, will be caught in the blast."

"Please don't. Seriously, please, please don't."

"Mr. Six, no more! Please! I'm begging you!"

As Alice and I exchange glares, Tillis and Viper desperately try to stop us.

Deciding it's too dangerous to leave things as they are, Tillis quickly issues orders to those around her.

"Snow, rally the other knights and soldiers and apprehend those two… But do it as calmly as possible. Try not to harm them or cause any unnecessary fuss."

Snow flinches at her orders, and I totally understand.

For the most part, she just does as she's told. But rarely—extremely rarely—she shows off her admirable side.

Given the circumstances, I can't really blame her. I'd probably comply with Tillis's commands if I were in her shoes.

"Y-Your Highness… I don't mean to disobey a direct order, but… this woman, Viper, is a very good person—rare for a demon… And she's great with paperwork, and she can fight, too! Killing her would be a terrible waste. She's much more valuable alive…"

"That's enough."

The one who cuts off Snow's desperate appeal is Viper herself.

"I'm touched by your gesture, Ms. Snow. Thinking back on it, I did nothing but cause problems for you in Hideout City. But it's really all right. For a long time, many feared me simply because I was the Demon Lord's daughter. They weren't even afraid of me but of my title. Once I came here, however, my abilities were properly appreciated, and I was valued for the merit of my contributions. Now the very people I worked alongside have come to my defense. I couldn't be happier. I couldn't ask for anything else… So please don't look so sad."

With that, Viper makes her way to Alice and the others.

When I glance in that direction, I meet Alice's gaze, and she nods as if to say, *Leave the rest to me.*

…I *can* trust you, right?

"Viper, you're special. From what I've seen, you're extremely capable and not at all a moron like the Combat Agents."

It's irritating that she needs to diss me even now, but since she's not wrong, I stay quiet.

As the knights and soldiers tensely watch the exchange, Alice holds something out.

"This manual contains instructions for how to use this item. What you do with it is up to you. You've come this far, so you might as well show them what a Demon Lord's made of."

After accepting the item from Alice, Viper skims the instruction manual.

I sidle up to Viper as she reads and peer over her shoulder, but the words are written in this planet's language. I can't make heads or tails of it.

After finishing the manual, she turns to Alice and me with a faintly embarrassed smile.

Then, she leaps up to the roof of a house.

High above the city, with the moon at her back, the beautiful young woman clearly stands out from everything else.

The various spectators who have been vaguely looking at our direction can't help but stare at her.

Viper locks eyes with me, and then, with a deadly serious expression, she says:

"I am Viper—daughter of the former Demon Lord Mehlmehl and current reigning Demon Lord!"

Suddenly indulging in a bit of melodrama, Viper continues to draw everyone's attention, flourishing her cape.

Holding up the object she received from Alice, she continues:

"The demon invasion of the human lands was wrought by my hand and mine alone. Using the secret brainwashing magic known only to the Demon Lords, I forced my ignorant and gullible populace to fight to this point. However..."

...Oh, she's doing the thing where the villain spills the beans on their evil plan for no apparent reason.

"Those men there, the Combat Agents of the Kisaragi Corporation, foiled every last one of my plans. In a final bid for survival, I carried out terrorist attacks to cover my escape, but it seems they've messed that up for me, too... Yes, the explosions and the monster attacks were all my doing..."

Alice watches the display with a look of glee. Is this really gonna be okay?

I'm getting really, really worried all of a sudden.

"Rather than die at the hands of you pathetic humans, I would sooner end my own life! Witness how a true Demon Lord dies…"

Shit, this sort of thing never ends well…!

I try to run to her, but Viper pulls something that looks like a pin from the device she's holding…

"Witness my power! Come, arc of the firmament! Let the earth tremble! Midgar's Lightning!"

A concussive blast shakes the sky, and Viper vanishes in an intense flash of light.

"Well done! Look at that, Six! She went out in a blaze of glory! What a truly amazing display of evil! That was incredible!"

"You idiot! I should've known… Damn you and your obsession with self-destructing…! I can't believe I was stupid enough to trust you…!"

9

It's been a week since the celebration.

After Viper went out with a bang, a hysterical Heine and I got some time off. We've been spending our days in a stupor.

Of course, in my case, even without getting the time off, it's not like I do any work.

Alice really is responsible for the outcome this time around, but I understand her on an intellectual level. Though I hate to admit it, the cold, unfeeling android is right.

I guess if the only other option was to be executed as a lowly prisoner while the masses howl for blood, it's better to leave an impact and keep the pride of a Demon Lord intact.

Yeah, yeah, I know all that.

And I know that, in order to end the long-standing war, there needs to be some sort of scapegoat...

"...Hey, Heine. 'Eyes of Red, Mane of Night. The Unrivaled King of All-Consuming Flame'... What monster does that sound like to you?"

"...Sounds like a description for a dark god or a god of destruction or something. Don't ask me. I'm not good at using my head."

The puzzles are still confusing as hell, but I'm determined to finish this shitty game.

I'd rather not ask for Alice's help, but at this rate, I might need it.

"...Looks like *dark god* and *god of destruction* are both wrong. *Sigh*, I died again..."

As I lay on the office sofa, I toss the game console aside.

Heine is lazily draped against the chair where Viper used to sit and do her work.

"...I wonder how long I have off... If Mr. Destroyer's getting hungry, I should probably return to work as soon as possible..."

I guess she still doesn't know the truth about Mr. Destroyer. It's more entertaining to watch her act as though he's alive, though, so I'm not about to tell her.

...As I let out a loud yawn, I hear something come in over the intercom.

"All Kisaragi personnel, please assemble in the square. A new mutant has arrived from headquarters. They will now make their introduction. Make sure all of you attend."

At Alice's sudden announcement, I let out a brief "...Oh, right."

"Oops. I forgot I'd requested mutant reinforcements from HQ."

"With all these forces at your disposal, you still need more?"

Heine asks this, but no, that's not it.

I had requested they send over Panda Man or Koala Man because a certain someone had a thing for cute creatures.

But it's pointless now.

"I guess I should go welcome them since it was my request..."

I can't muster up any enthusiasm, but I don't really have a choice.

At least Panda Man and Koala Man are soothing just to be around.

Maybe they're what we need most right now.

Heine and I drag our lethargic bodies out of the office and somehow make our way to the square.

We arrive to find everyone else already waiting.

"Hey, Alice, who did they send? Panda Man or Koala Man?"

"Huh? Those two are too popular to send to a backwater rock like this."

I can't help but deflate at Alice's quick reply.

I was going to bury my face in Panda Man's plush belly, but it seems I won't even get to indulge in that little bit of happiness.

I slump in front of the assembled Combat Agents and vaguely glance in the direction of our new mutant recruit.

The mutant is dressed in a full bodysuit that looks a bit like a motorcycle outfit.

And unusually for a mutant, they're wearing a helmet that covers their whole face, much like the ones given to us Combat Agents.

Based on the few features that I can see poking through the suit, it seems this mutant is a woman.

Maybe I should start giving Alice more credit...

As tears flow down Heine's cheeks, the mutant—who is only wearing a sleeve on her left arm for some reason—speaks in a voice that sounds oddly familiar.

*   *   *

"Hello, everyone. It's a pleasure to meet you all. I am the mutant Snake Woman. I've been sent from Kisaragi Corporation headquarters to aid in your efforts… I'm fairly confident in my ability to process paperwork, and my hobby is…"

Though she's supposed to be addressing everyone in attendance, I feel her looking directly at me as she speaks.

"…solving puzzles in video games."

And with that, the corners of her mouth curl up into a radiant smile.

Epilogue

It's the day after the new leader's arrival.

We've managed to hand out home assignments and jobs to the demon settlers, and Hideout City is starting to develop a real sense of community.

Last night, we were also able to squeak by without explaining much of anything because everyone got so wasted at the welcome party, but right now, Alice is surrounded by Combat Agents all demanding answers.

"Hey, shrimp, you might have squeezed out a happy ending this time, but clue us in next time, will ya?"

"Good job this time, runt. Great job with Snake Woman, by the way!"

"Don't let this get to your head, tiny. Also, go to Lady Lilith and get some big boobs installed."

Having had her hair thoroughly ruffled and her cheeks tugged and squeezed by the Combat Agents, Alice is starting to look really pissed off.

"You guys are too stupid to help with a bluff. I had already gotten Tillis to agree to a mock public execution… But sure enough, in came Six, the one-brain-cell wonder, eager to screw everything up…"

"Okay, I'll admit that was pretty clever of you, pip-squeak. But seriously, tell us next time. If you repeat yourself a hundred times or so, even we won't mess things up."

"I'll be honest, I still don't really follow, but it all worked out, didn't it? Great! That means you can get back to work. We're counting on ya for the reports since we don't know the language and all."

"Hey, Alice, since the war's over, you should stop acting like our boss and show us some proper respect!"

Unable to listen a second longer, Alice finally snaps. Her expression becomes devoid of all emotion, and she speaks in a mechanical voice.

"Damage to core unit detected. Company Secret Preservation protocol initiated. Self-destruction imminent. All nearby residents and Kisaragi operatives are to leave the immediate area at once. I repeat—"

"Wait, Alice, that's not funny! Don't even joke about that! It's scary as hell!"

"Okay, okay, we were wrong, Alice! Stop with that creepy robot stuff!"

"You're kidding about self-destructing, right?! You're just messing with us, right?! Please don't be mad at us, Ms. Alice!"

From the office window, I watch the other Combat Agents drop everything to try to get back on Alice's good side. I then flop onto the sofa with my game console in hand.

"Hey, Vi. What does this mean to you…? 'Gale above, glacier below, and lightning storm behind. Thou must speak my name!'"

"Perhaps it's the name of a country rather than a creature? I've heard the country of Vivimunt in the tundra region is plagued by typhoons and lightning strikes."

As Viper explains the answer to me, Rose is taking a nap with her head on Viper's lap.

I enter my response while Viper scratches her pen along her paper…

"Fool, begone! Thou shalt begin this dungeon anew!"

"Vi…! It didn't work! What should I do? Do I really have to do all that again…?"

"Oh, was that wrong? I'm so sorry! Please forgive me! Once I finish sorting the paperwork, I'll play up to that point for you!"

On the day I thought I had lost Vi, the item Alice had handed over to her was a harmless flash grenade made for stage shows. All it did was emit sound and light. The note Alice had attached instructed Viper to use the device to pretend to blow herself up, then hide using Agent Ten's optical camo device. The original plan had been to do a holographic public execution. Since Combat Agents are idiots who suck at lying, the two of them had planned everything out in secret. For screwing that plan up, I won myself a lengthy lecture from Alice and Tillis.

While I ruminate on the events of that day, I hear:

"…Hrmph, you've already moved on to a new woman? You really are scum."

After barging into the office without so much as a knock, Snow furrows her brow upon seeing Viper and me together.

Oh yeah, she hasn't been clued in yet.

"Um, Mr. Six, shouldn't we tell Ms. Snow…?"

"Nah, no need, my dear Viper. She's just a gold digger who'd probably sell you out for a big enough bribe."

Hearing me address Viper by her new nickname, Snow perks up.

"…Did you just call her 'Viper'?"

"On my planet, there are different species of snakes like boa constrictors and vipers. Since she's Snake Woman, I'm calling her Viper."

Hearing that, Snow frowns in disgust.

"You really are a piece of work. To address this new woman by the same name as that poor girl who gave her life to fulfill her duty as the Demon Lord… Sure, I bullied her every day on behalf of the soldiers who lost their lives, but I did respect her, both as a leader and as a person. And yet you…"

"U-um, Ms. Snow, please. That's quite enough…"

Viper blushes at the compliments, but Snow snaps in her direction.

"I don't remember saying you could address me as Ms. Snow!"

"I-I'm sorry!"

Snow scratches at her head in irritation, then turns back to me.

"But forget all that. There's actually a reason I'm here."

With that, she straightens up.

"Please hire me to work at Kisaragi!"

…

"Huh? You do know that if we strip you of your knighthood, you'll have nothing left…right?"

"There'll be plenty left! Wait, that's not what I—! Look…the truth is, Her Highness has given me quite the lecture for this incident… It seems I might finally be getting fired…"

Actually, I've already heard this part from Tillis.

She herself asked me to add not only Grimm and Rose but also Snow to my ranks.

Which is why her transfer is already a done deal, but…

"If you'll address me as Mr. Six and provide me some sort of sexy service every day, I'll consider it."

"M-Mr. Six, th-that's going a little too far… And Ms. Snow's termination is probably my fault…"

Viper interjects at my proposal, but it seems Snow's realized something.

"W-wait, as a mutant, isn't Snake Woman higher up the chain of command than Six?! M-Ms. Snake Woman, please add me to the Kisaragi ranks!"

"Hey! You little…!"

It's true; with her competence and strength, Viper's been hired on as a Leader class.

I—I mean, she's a former Demon Lord, and she's already used to managing people. I'm not at all bothered by her appointment. Really, I'm not.

...Just as I was trying to convince myself of that fact—

"Emergency alert! All Kisaragi operatives are to halt their tasks and assemble in the conference room."

—Alice's announcement rings out, accompanied by the emergency alarm.

Perking my ears to figure out what's happening...

"Our enemy, the kingdom of Toris, has been wiped out. I repeat, all available operatives are to assemble in the conference room."

AFTERWORD

Thank you for picking up Volume 5 of *Combatants Will Be Dispatched!* I'm your author, Natsume Akatsuki.

We've finally made it to Volume 5. When the first volume came out, whether additional volumes would come out or not would be predicated on sales, but thanks to you, dear reader, I've managed to publish more. Many thanks, many thanks!

This volume's got a pretty high dose of serious topics and a hefty dose of low-level Combat Agents, but from now on, they're going to be staying behind at the hideout, so I'm glad I was able to let them have some screen time before the end of the Demon Lord arc.

If this were *Konosuba*, I suppose this would be the end of the road, but for the *Combatants* series, the fantasy elements are just getting started.

This volume is a sort of milestone as the main cast is finally assembled.

Exploring the mysteries behind Rose's origins and the various O-Parts scattered around. The development and exploration of the planet. This is just the beginning of getting the actual invasion started.

The end goal of this story isn't the defeat of the Demon Lord, so he sort of wound up being defeated pretty easily, but I think, someday, stories of his personal life and incidents might be told...

I suppose there won't be that much demand, so it might only show up as Viper's memories or something. Nothing to be done about that.

Also, there's going to be a really important announcement about this series soon.

I'll say ahead of time it's not a drama CD.

I'm not trying to be coy, but Sneaker will be making the announcement soon, so stay tuned!

So anyway, the reason I was able to get this volume out the door despite getting really cornered by deadlines is thanks to the help of the illustrator, Kakao Lanthanum, along with my managing editor K, and everyone else in the editing department, as well as many other people.

I offer my thanks to everyone involved in the publishing process.

And of course, this has become a habitual show of gratitude, but to everyone who picked up this volume, deep, deep thanks!

Natsume Akatsuki